Suddenly the silence of the cavern was broken by a deep sigh, a sigh so desolate that he glanced round expecting the very walls to drip with tears. His startled movements dislodged a shower of pebbles. He knew at once that the creature who sighed had heard him.

A whisper came from the chasm and echoed around the cave. *"Who? Who comes at last? Who comes?"*

Spread-eagled against the rock, Kerish was silent.

"Who comes . . . ? My key!" The voice cracked with anger. *"You have come to steal my key! My power, my life! You shall not have it."* The voice grew louder. *"I will take you down into my darkness."*

From the black chasm rose two hands, whiter than the faces of the walking dead. Blindly, they groped for Kerish and the cavern was filled with desperate whispering.

"No, my life, my key, you shall never take it!"

GERALDINE HARRIS has written several books for young adults. She lives in Oxford, England.

SEVEN CITADELS ♦ PART III

THE DEAD KINGDOM

GERALDINE HARRIS

LAUREL-LEAF BOOKS

LAUREL-LEAF BOOKS bring together under a single imprint outstanding works of fiction and nonfiction particularly suitable for young adult readers, both in and out of the classroom. Charles F. Reasoner, Professor Emeritus of Children's Literature and Reading, New York University, is consultant to this series.

Published by
Dell Publishing Co., Inc.
1 Dag Hammarskjold Plaza
New York, New York 10017

Laurel-Leaf Library ® TM 766734, Dell Publishing Co., Inc.

ISBN: 0-440-91810-3

RL: 6.7

Reprinted by arrangement with Greenwillow Books, a division of William Morrow & Company, Inc.

Printed in the United States of America

October 1987

10 9 8 7 6 5 4 3 2 1

WFH

THE HOUSE OF THE EMPERORS

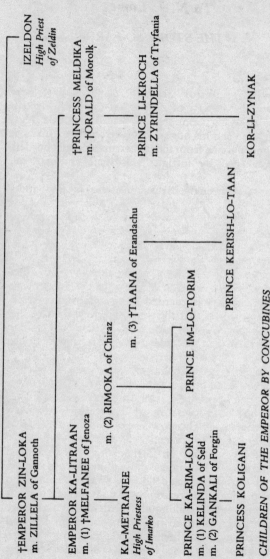

†EMPEROR ZIN-LOKA
m. ZILLELA of Gannoth

IZELDON
High Priest
of Zeldin

EMPEROR KA-LITRAAN
m. (1) †MELFANEE of Jenoza
m. (2) RIMOKA of Chiraz
m. (3) †TAANA of Erandachu

†PRINCESS MELDIKA
m. †ORALD of Morolk

PRINCE LI-KROCH
m. ZYRINDELLA of Tryfania

KA-METRANEE
High Priestess
of Imarko

PRINCE IM-LO-TORIM

PRINCE KERISH-LO-TAAN

KOR-LI-ZYNAK

PRINCE KA-RIM-LOKA
m. (1) KELINDA of Seld
m. (2) GANKALI of Forgin

PRINCESS KOLIGANI

CHILDREN OF THE EMPEROR BY CONCUBINES

1 By †VALDISSA

2 By FOLLEA

3 By †MELZEEN (wife of the Governor of Tryfania)

LORD JERENAC

LORD FOROLLKIN

ZYRINDELLA

THE STORY SO FAR

The beginning of the story *Seven Citadels* is told in *Prince of the Godborn*. In the east of Zindar lies the great Galkian Empire ruled by the Godborn; the descendants of Zeldin, the Gentle God and his human consort, the Lady Imarko. Galkis is under attack from the barbarians along its borders and is weakened by intrigue and strife amongst the Godborn.

An alliance between the barbarians of the Five Kingdoms and the Brigands of Fangmere brings a new crisis and the High Priest Izeldon sees an ancient prophesy of an imprisoned Saviour as the only hope for Galkis. He asks Prince Kerish-lo-Taan, a son of the Emperor by a slave-girl from Erandachu, to go out into Zindar and search for this promised Saviour. Izeldon reveals that the only way to free the Saviour is to win the seven keys to the gates of his prison, but each key is guarded by an immortal sorcerer. The Emperor insists that the impulsive Kerish share his quest with his sensible half-brother, Lord Forollkin, and the two young men cross the Dirian Sea to visit King Elmandis of Ellerinonn, the first of the sorcerers.

Elmandis proves to be a philosopher-king ruling a gentle people dedicated to bringing peace and beauty to Zindar. He sees Kerish's coming as a disaster, because a sorcerer who gives up his key loses immortality. Kerish has to face a grim ordeal and use all his powers of argument to persuade the noble Elmandis to surrender the first key.

The second sorcerer is Ellandellore, the estranged younger brother of Elmandis, whose domain is Cheransee, the Isle of Illusions. Ellandellore is a crazed child who cannot be persuaded by reason to give up the key that has trapped him in eternal childhood. Kerish plays a nightmare game with Ellandellore to trick him out of his key and barely escapes with his life. Elmandis can now help his brother to grow up at last. He tells Kerish to look for the third sorcerer far north in the Ultimate Mountains and sends them on their way with a mysterious travelling companion: the ugly and insolent Gidjabolgo.

In *The Children of the Wind* Kerish, Forollkin and Gidjabolgo the Forgite buy a passage north, through the marshes of Lan-Pin-Fria, on the ship of a Merchant-Hunter. After a dangerous and eventful journey, during which Kerish acquires the marsh cat Lilahnee, the travellers reach the Forbidden Hill. In spite of warnings to go no further, they cross the hill and discover a strange ruined city, before being overwhelmed by a snowstorm. The travellers wake in Tir-Zulmar, the mountain citadel of the third sorcerer, to find that the first two keys have been stolen. Kerish confronts the third sorcerer and discovers that she is a woman from the island of Gannoth. The sorceress Sendaaka tells Kerish how she quarrelled with and left her husband Saroc, the fourth sorcerer, and about the tragic death of their only daughter. The two sorcerers can never be re-united unless one of them gives up their key. Kerish persuades Sendaaka to lend him her key and return the first two keys. He promises to convince Saroc to give up his key and ask Sendaaka's forgiveness, without revealing that she has already yielded her key. If he fails, Kerish will have to return Sendaaka's key and his quest will be over.

To reach the citadel of Saroc, which lies in the Queendom of Seld, the companions will have to cross the plains of Erandachu. Sendaaka warns them that they are bound to meet the Erandachi, the Children of the Wind, who worship her as their 'Mountain Goddess'. Half-way across the plains, the travellers are captured by the Sheyasa tribe, whose chieftain, Tayeb, proves to be Kerish's uncle. They are welcomed into the tribe by Tayeb's daughter, Gwerath, a priestess of the Mountain Goddess, who takes an immediate liking to Forollkin.

Tayeb wants Kerish and Forollkin to help him against his enemies within the tribe and forbids them to leave. Forollkin's skill and courage win him an honoured place as a warrior, but Kerish is made a priest of the Mountain Goddess and Gidjabolgo a slave. Kerish is eager to attract Gwerath's attention and jealous of Forollkin's status as a warrior. The tension between the two brothers, which has been mounting throughout their journey, erupts when Kerish wins the right to be a warrior by fighting Forollkin. He nearly kills his brother, but Forollkin forgives him and their resolve to escape from the Sheyasa is strengthened. The escape is only possible with Gwerath's help and they are forced to take her with them.

Arriving in Seld, the four travellers encounter its ruler, Queen Pellameera, and are invited to court. There they are told about the horrors of Saroc's citadel and Kerish learns that his father is dead. The quest is now more urgent than ever and Kerish and his companions set out to win the key of the fourth sorcerer. The story continues in *The Dead Kingdom*.

Chapter One

THREE tents were pitched on the lowest slope of the White Hills of Lamoth; one was for the Queen's favourite, Lord Djezaney; the second was for the strangers he was escorting through Seld — the Prince of Galkis, his half-brother Forollkin and the Forgite, who followed them like a dog, begging for scraps between snarls. The third tent lodged the Galkians' cousin, the silver-haired Erandachi princess, who scandalized her Seldian escort by carrying weapons and dressing like a boy. At the close of a long, light evening, Djezaney's servants were about to serve the meal which they had prepared over the camp fire. A page drew a ewer of water from a nearby spring, picked and crushed some flowers to scent it, and knelt before the Princess offering to wash her hands. As usual, she refused, but Prince Kerish-lo-Taan submitted gracefully. Lord Djezaney let the boy wash and dry his good hand, swearing when the napkin caught in one of his rings. The page looked round for the Prince's brother but Lord Forollkin was kneeling at the bottom of the slope where the lush grass ended and the Red Waste began.

The young Galkian ran a few grains of sand through his fingers. They were as hot as new ashes. In the distance gloomed the citadel of Saroc. On their peaceful journey through the quiet Seldian countryside, Djezaney had maliciously related all the tales that he could remember or invent about the horrors of Tir-Tonar. At least they provided a good excuse for forbidding Gwerath to come with them into the Red Waste. The Princess had sworn that she would never forgive Forollkin if he didn't change his mind. Secure in the belief that he was acting for her own good, Forollkin had taken this calmly. He smiled at the memory of her anger but, as he watched the red sand trickling through his fingers, his thoughts turned to a red-haired woman.

He listed the reasons why he should find the Queen of Seld contemptible, but her image danced through his thoughts. Every detail of her grace seemed to have hooked itself to him and could not be torn away without pain.

The timid voice of the page, asking if he wished to eat, roused Forollkin. Smiling at the boy, the tall Galkian got up and walked towards the tents. Cushions had been heaped on the grass and an embroidered cloth spread for the silver dishes and goblets. The sight of a lady eating in public had so distressed the Seldians on the first night of their journey, that Gwerath had reluctantly agreed to retire to her tent during meals. That night she did so with little grace and scowled at Forollkin to make sure that he knew he was being ignored.

Kerish-lo-Taan was leaning against one of the white boulders that gave the hills their name. Looking down at his brother's calm face and startling eyes Forollkin wished he could imagine what Kerish was thinking and feeling; wished for a moment that he could understand what it was like to be anyone else, to be Gwerath, or Gidjabolgo, or the Queen of Seld . . .

"Your dinner's getting sour," said Gidjabolgo.

The Forgite lounged on a pile of cushions next to Kerish, with the green shape of the marsh cat stretched out between them. Djezaney's hand was already dripping with honey as he nibbled a sticky cake. Forollkin sat down beside him and took the cover off one of the silver dishes. Inside, delicate slivers of meat were swamped by a rich, sweet sauce.

"Do you never cook anything in Seld without pouring honey all over it?" asked Forollkin.

Djezaney licked the crumbs from his lips. "Women's food is different. Men like their food over-sweet. Custom tells us so."

"Must you always follow custom?"

"The Queen is a great upholder of custom," answered Djezaney, "and I am the Queen's Favourite."

"One of them," said Gidjabolgo unkindly, "and what Queen would not uphold customs that tie the men of Seld to her skirts?"

To keep the peace, Kerish asked hastily, "How long has Seld been a Queendom?"

Djezaney shrugged. "Do you expect a man to know? Ask one of the scholars of Trykis."

"I expect you to know." Kerish picked a slice of meat off his plate to feed to the marsh cat. "The Queen did mention that you could read."

"A rare privilege." Djezaney's smile was not a pleasant one. "Well then . . . there have been Queens on the throne of Seld for six hundred years. Once, the land was divided into a Northern and a Southern realm, each ruled by a King. Six hundred years ago the Kings were pious men. The King of the North thought himself the incarnation of Melkiniak, the northern god, and the King of the South claimed to be the son of Kilmenior, the southern god. Each asserted that his god was supreme and it came to a long and bloody war between them. Seld was devastated. The King of the North had married Bekeena, the sister of the King of the South. She tried to make a peace between them and, during a truce, brought them together to talk. When she saw that they could not agree and that the war would begin again, Bekeena poisoned them both and took the crown. She banished gods from Seld and razed their temples, all except Trykis, the prison of the Queen's sisters."

Forollkin took a mouthful of tart wine. "So now there are Queens and Seld prospers."

Djezaney nodded. "We are all as plump and peaceful as caged birds, fed by the Queen's favour."

Forollkin drained his goblet. "Well it's not a life I'd take to."

"Then, from what I hear," answered Djezaney, "you'd better not return to Galkis, now that a woman rules your Empire."

3

"The Empress Rimoka merely advises her son," said Kerish stiffly. "She does not rule."

"I bow to your Highness' superior knowledge. Now if you will forgive me . . . "

Djezaney retired to his tent to re-curl his long black hair with the tongs that had been heated in the ashes of the camp fire.

"If I were Queen Pellameera," murmured Gidjabolgo, "I wouldn't trust my favourite further than I could sniff his scent."

"I don't think she does," said Kerish, as the marsh cat licked some sauce from his hands. "Perhaps she enjoys a whiff of danger."

"Gidjabolgo, are you sure you want to come with us tomorrow?" asked Forollkin suddenly. "If only a tenth of Djezaney's tales are true . . . "

"I'll take my chance with the sorcerer," said Gidjabolgo. "Unlike the Princess, at least I'm given a choice."

"You know as well as we do why she mustn't come," answered Kerish. "I know why you think so," agreed Gidjabolgo, "and I also know why *I* think that she should come."

At dawn, Kerish, Forollkin and Gidjabolgo set out on foot across the hot sand. Gwerath did not emerge from her tent to watch them go but Djezaney stood at the edge of the grass, still wrapped in his velvet bed-gown, with his face unpainted and his hands bare of rings.

"I will wait for you for three days. May the Queen's favour go with you!" It sounded more like a curse than a good wish.

Almost as soon as they entered the Red Waste, Lilahnee began hopping from leg to leg. She licked her paws and mewed in distress but when Kerish took her back to the camp she refused to stay there without him.

"Ignore her," ordered Forollkin. "Her paws are tough enough: she's only trying to catch attention."

As they walked southwards, with Lilahnee limping behind, the cool dawn of the hills was replaced by a fierce heat.

"Look at the sky," whispered Kerish. "It's changed."

Above them the cloudless arch of the sky had darkened from warm blue to a heavy red.

"It's closer," muttered Gidjabolgo.

The travellers felt trapped between the red sand and the red sky and there seemed no space to move or breathe.

"This is Saroc's realm," said Kerish. "He shapes it to his will."

For an hour they walked in silence, pausing every so often to drink from the leathern water-flask that Gidjabolgo carried slung across his shoulder. The flat sands were broken by an occasional dune and sometimes the travellers stumbled over slabs that might once have been part of a road and the stumps of long-dead trees.

"What's that?" asked Gidjabolgo suddenly and then they all noticed a green object sticking up above the sand. Lilahnee bounded forward to sniff at it while the others approached more cautiously. The stone was cracked and chipped but they could still make out the shape of a wide-mouthed, leaping fish.

"Perhaps it was part of a fountain," suggested Kerish, "when the Red Waste was a garden."

Something had caught the Forgite's eye and he scrabbled in the sand that had drifted against the stone.

"Gold!" He held up a bracelet of gold and crystal, set with a single, long red hair.

"Stop it, Gidjabolgo!" cried Kerish but as he spoke the sand slithered away to reveal the owner of the bracelet crouched beside the choked fountain.

The dry air and hot sand had preserved the body well and scraps of gaudy clothing and a few blonde curls still clung to the desiccated skin. Gidjabolgo scraped his hands against his thighs.

"This must be the foolish Lord they spoke of back in Lamoth. The father of the Queen's daughters."

"Theligarn," murmured Forollkin.

"Cover him again," ordered Kerish, "but perhaps we should take this bracelet back to Pellameera."

"Give it to me," said Forollkin, and he slipped it on his own wrist.

"How do you think he died?" asked Gidjabolgo,

stooping down to peer into what was left of the face.

"His right arm has been torn off . . . " began Forollkin, "and the chest . . . " Abruptly he knelt and heaped the red sand over the withered body. "Come on. Keep walking, but, by Zeldin, I wish it wasn't so hot!"

Kerish delved into his tunic and drew out the Jewel of Zeldin. Its pellucid light seemed unaffected by the red glare of the oppressive sky and it was cool to the touch. He held it against his forehead for a moment and then passed it to Forollkin and Gidjabolgo. It seemed to help all of them shake off the worst effects of the heat.

For five hours they walked steadily on towards the Citadel of Saroc. Tir-Tonar was enclosed by walls of smooth crimson stone, twelve times the height of a man. The travellers could see no entrance but, as they came closer, they noticed dark patches against the crimson. These might have been windows but they were irregular in shape and Kerish could have sworn that they sometimes moved. Forollkin dismissed it as a trick of the shimmering heat.

Gidjabolgo's keen ears first heard the noise, or perhaps it was Lilahnee. She began to growl and the fur stood up in spikes along her back. Kerish put his arm around her neck but she refused to be soothed.

"Do you hear it?" demanded the Forgite. "A kind of crying, very thin and shrill." They walked forward slowly and the noise increased until they could all hear it. They entered the gigantic shadow of Tir-Tonar and, free of the glare of the red sun, Kerish looked up at the walls.

"Zeldin and Imarko!"

As if it had heard the Prince's appalled whisper, one of the patches of darkness broke from the wall and plunged towards them. In that second the travellers realized that they were hearing the voices of the guardians of Tir-Tonar.

Forollkin tore off his cloak and wrapped it round his left arm as a shield. He drew his sword and ordered the others to get behind him but Kerish stayed at his side, dagger in hand, and Lilahnee crouched at their feet, spitting bravely. Black and crimson wings beat at the air, the creature shrieked and the sound was almost too high for them to hear, but it made their heads ring. Kerish had a brief impression of a scaled snout, a long row of teeth and horribly human arms that ended in clawed hands. Forollkin slashed at the creature but it swerved towards Kerish and knocked him to his knees with a blow of its wing. The Prince ducked to avoid the raking claws and lunged blindly with his dagger. He missed but Forollkin brought his sword crashing down on the creature's head. Its black scales turned the blade and the arms stretched out again for Kerish.

Growling with rage, Lilahnee sprang at the creature's throat. The white arms closed around her and the claws thrust deep into her green fur. Forollkin hacked at the guardian's vulnerable wings but it would not let go. The marsh cat sank her teeth into the creature's throat. With a bubbling scream the guardian struggled upwards, carrying Lilahnee clutched to its heart.

Kerish saw the creature claw at the green furred back. Then, with a triumphant screech, it shook the marsh cat free. Lilahnee fell to the ground, writhed and lay still. Kerish would have run to her but Forollkin grabbed his arm, shouting, "Stand back to back!"

Two more shadows swooped down from the walls.

The three men leaned against each other, braced for another attack, as the creatures circled them.

"Aim for their throats!" ordered Forollkin.

Screaming mouths and beating wings seemed to surround them. Gidjabolgo slashed out wildly and one of the guardians caught the Forgite's cloak between its jaws, dragging him forward. Kerish hacked at its pale arms till the creature dropped the cloak and flew upwards again. Forollkin thanked Zeldin for the thick cloak wrapped around his arm when one of the guardians ducked under a thrust and clawed at his left side.

It was Kerish who noticed the sound of hoofbeats. In a moment's respite he twisted round and saw a pony galloping towards them. He knew its rider by the silver hair streaming out behind her. He parried a slashing claw as he watched two of the guardians fly towards her. The pony reared but Gwerath kept her seat and drew her dagger. The guardians hovered over her, driving the pony wild with panic. Then one of them swooped. Gwerath struck up at it

7

but its long claws raked her pony's shoulder. Screaming, the pony fell and rolled on the red sand. Gwerath was thrown clear and Kerish raced towards her.

Forollkin struck a tremendous blow that half-severed the wing of his attacker. The creature flapped clumsily away, leaving a trail of blood and feathers.

"The girl!" gasped Gidjabolgo.

In seconds Forollkin had understood the danger.

"Guard my back," he ordered, throwing down his sword. He reached for his bow and fitted an arrow to the string.

Dazed by her fall, Gwerath fumbled for the dagger which had been knocked from her hand. Then she heard a rush of wings and shielded her face. A moment later, Kerish threw himself in front of her, clasping his dagger with both hands. He heard the whine of an arrow as it struck the first guardian in the throat. The creature soared upwards and circled slowly, trying to pluck out the arrow with its clumsy hands.

The second guardian was on Kerish before his brother could fire again. The Prince knelt in the shadow of the black and crimson wings and the long arms reached beyond him to strike at Gwerath. Kerish stabbed upwards with all his strength, through the feathered breast and into the heart. The creature gave one last piercing scream as he pulled out the dagger black with blood. Kerish gripped Gwerath and rolled with her to one side as the guardian crumpled to the sand.

Still plucking at the arrow in its throat, the first creature swooped clumsily down but when Kerish held up the dripping dagger it sheered away and spiralled up into the red sky. Then the Prince heard Gidjabolgo's voice. One of the creatures still hovered above him, screaming angrily, and the Forgite's dagger was no match for the sweeping wings and clawed hands. Forollkin dropped his bow and snatched up his sword. Kerish raced towards them and drops of blood burned on the sand. The guardian's dark eyes flickered towards the Prince and, with a last slash at Gidjabolgo, it flew up and away from them, back to Tir-Tonar.

8

"Forollkin, Gidjabolgo . . . are you hurt?"

Leaning on his sword, Forollkin wearily shook his head. Gidjabolgo complained of a clawed arm but, though they bled profusely, the scratches were not deep. The ramparts were black with guardians but the sky was free of them.

"They seem to fear my dagger," said Kerish. "Their own heart's blood . . ."

Gwerath walked unsteadily to his side. "Are we safe from them now?"

"I don't know. Perhaps the blood is poisonous to them . . ."

Forollkin's angry voice interrupted him. "Gwerath! What in Zeldin's name are you doing here? I left you safely with Djezaney . . ."

"I don't want to be safe!" shouted Gwerath. "Kerish said that this could be my quest too, so why should I be left behind? Why won't you let me help you?"

"What help could you be?" asked Forollkin witheringly. "Gidjabolgo will escort you back to the White Hills while we . . ."

"Not me!" exclaimed the Forgite. "I'm staying by the Prince's dagger. All forward, or all back."

"I won't allow it," snapped Forollkin. "Kerish, you tell . . ."

Kerish was not there. He was kneeling beside the fallen marsh cat. Forollkin's anger suddenly drained away.

"I suppose you'll have to stay with us, Gwerath, but from now on you obey my orders."

Gwerath nodded meekly and all of them walked towards Kerish.

"She wasn't quite dead when I reached her," Kerish said quietly. "She snarled at me. She didn't seem to know me."

Forollkin laid a tentative hand on his brother's shoulder.

"She died bravely, protecting you."

Kerish stiffened.

"Do you think that makes it any easier?"

Forollkin silently cursed himself for always saying the wrong thing.

"I only meant that she would have wanted . . ."

Kerish cut him short.

9

"We must bury her before we go on. Gwerath's pony too."

They crossed to where the pony lay, its open eyes reflecting the red sky.

"Is there anything you need from the saddle-bags?" asked Forollkin.

Gwerath shook her head. Close to the pony lay the guardian that Kerish had killed.

"Look!" The Prince had knelt and was ruffling the feathers at its throat. "It wears a collar."

They all stooped and saw the silver collar inscribed in Seldian.

"Acanoth," read Kerish. "Do you think that's its name? Forollkin, would you bring Lilahnee here? We'll bury them together."

"But one of those creatures killed her!" protested Gwerath.

"Please, Forollkin."

They dug a shallow pit around the dead guardian and dragged the pony into it. Forollkin brought Lilahnee's limp green body and laid it on a bed of black and crimson feathers. Kerish closed the golden eyes but he would not touch her matted fur. He threw the first handful of sand over her and then walked away. Forollkin and Gidjabolgo filled in the grave.

Kerish held up his blood-stained dagger and, keeping close together, they approached the walls of Tir-Tonar. In the shadow of the citadel it suddenly seemed cold and they stared up anxiously at the creatures that clung to unseen cracks in the crimson stone. The guardians continued their eerie shrieking, ruffled their wings and flexed their clawed hands, but they did not move from the summit of the walls. He glanced to left and right along the smooth curve of the crimson rampart but could see no entrance. The blood on his dagger was almost dry and he wondered how much longer it would keep the guardians back.

They set off, walking sunwise round the walls, bunched together and always looking upwards, waiting for a new attack. As the minutes passed, the guardians became more and more restless and Kerish ached with tension. Then, at last, they came to a great, dark crack in the crimson walls. It ran from the red sands to the very top of the ramparts and guardians were clinging all the way up.

"Through there?" whispered Gwerath, instinctively lifting her arms to shield her head. Forollkin nodded.

"I'll go first, follow me closely," said Kerish.

The lowest of the creatures was no more than five feet above their heads and one of its clawed hands hung loose against the crimson stone. With the Jewel of Zeldin in his left hand and the dagger in his right, Kerish half ran through the crack and the others stumbled after him with bowed heads. Every guardian along the walls gave a scream of desolation and rose in flight. Their wings darkened the sky and the travellers dropped to their knees, their hands clasped to their ears.

The screams stabbed at Kerish but after a moment he forced himself to hold the dagger steady and look up. The guardians were flying away from Tir-Tonar, dipping and circling over the Red Waste. The travellers were alone on a crimson terrace that seemed to encircle the citadel inside the ramparts. One by one they stood up and looked about them. At the heart of Tir-Tonar stood a slender tower but between the tower and the terrace stretched a vast, stone maze.

"I think we should make for that crimson tower," said Kerish.

"Through that?" Gidjabolgo pointed down at the maze. They were not high enough to see into more than a few of the passages and courtyards below but each of them had already filled the maze with private terrors.

"Well, forward then," said Forollkin, "before those creatures come back."

"No," Kerish turned to the Princess. "Gwerath. Please stay here, on the edge of the maze. I don't doubt your courage, but it would be better if you and the others didn't come any further. I'll go on alone to find Saroc."

"I won't be left behind," repeated Gwerath. "You would never have escaped from the Sheyasa without me. That gives me a right to share your quest!"

"No-one disputes that," said Kerish patiently, "but all

11

three of you should stay here while . . . "

"I'll not stay," growled Gidjabolgo. "I have a word or two to say to Saroc."

"And I'm not letting you face another sorcerer alone," protested Forollkin.

"But Gwerath mustn't . . . "

"She's come of her own free will," said Forollkin irritably. "There's no help for it now."

"Forollkin, I must order you to stay here and . . . "

"Order me? I seem to remember you swearing to obey *my* orders from now on."

"Yes, I remember too."

"Kerish, don't look like that. I didn't mean to remind you . . . " Forollkin rested a hand on his brother's shoulder. "But now we're all here, we ought to go on together. It's too dangerous to split up."

"If you've finished quarrelling," said Gidjabolgo, "look over there!"

He pointed towards the crimson tower. At its base lay a cloudlike mass of white, shot through with particles of gold.

"That wasn't there a moment ago!" exclaimed Forollkin.

"It's beautiful," whispered Gwerath. As she spoke the cloud seemed to crawl across the maze towards them.

"Beware of beauty in a sorcerer's citadel," said Gidjabolgo and they descended the narrow staircase that led into the maze.

At first there were only empty passages, walled and paved in polished crimson stone. It was almost bright enough to give back a clear reflection and Kerish walked in fear of his own image. As the passages twisted and divided, even Forollkin began to lose his sense of direction and faint, continuous rustlings, hissings and whisperings, never very close but never far off, made them all uneasy. They were not alone in the maze but whatever it was that made the noises was always on the other side of one of the high stone walls. They had walked for almost an hour before they came on a small courtyard and had their first sight of the creatures of the maze.

12

Stone flowers sprang up from cracks in the crimson floor and the air was rich with their scent. Amongst the flowers browsed the beasts of Saroc. Some of them were beautiful, but most were grotesque. One had an almost human face, framed by a green mane, and a sleek golden body; a second clattered across the stones on cloven hooves, its purple plumage streaked with white; a third had a spotted coat and a reptilian head, made ludicrous by its drooping ears; a fourth had a cat-like body but was beaked and winged like a bird of prey. Each beast wore a crimson collar inscribed with its name and they stared at the travellers with huge mournful eyes.

Kerish held up his bloodstained dagger, while the others got as close to him as they could. Opposite them the passage wound on but to reach it they would have to cross the courtyard.

"Let me go first," said Kerish and before Forollkin could disagree he had stepped amongst the stone flowers. A spiny beast with long, yellow tusks lumbered towards him. Kerish brandished the dagger and the creature paused for a moment in obvious puzzlement and then came on. Forollkin drew his sword and moved towards his brother but Kerish stretched out his left hand and then stood quite still. The beast sniffed at the Prince's fingers, then began to lick them, and a furred serpent coiled itself around his ankles, purring loudly. He smiled and sheathed his dagger.

"They're not going to harm us."

Forollkin was much more wary and backed away from the shaggy blue creature that gently butted his legs but Gwerath stroked the one-eyed beast that nuzzled her hand and Gidjabolgo ruffled the feathers of a two-headed bird. It took them some time to make their way across the courtyard, pushing aside the friendly beasts. Once all four travellers had reached the passage, the beasts seemed to lose interest and returned to browsing on the scent of the stone flowers. Gwerath looked back at them.

"Can Saroc be as cruel as the Seldians say if he keeps such gentle creatures?"

Nobody answered her and they walked quickly down the empty passageway, less troubled now by the noises of the

13

maze. After a few minutes they came to a second courtyard, with a floor that seemed to be made of black ice. As Forollkin tested its strength with one foot, the chill of the ice struck up, even through his boot. He beckoned to the others to follow him round the edge of the courtyard, leaning against one wall to stop themselves falling on the slippery black surface.

Half-way across, Kerish noticed a patch of clear ice. He knelt down to peer into the blackness and glimpsed a white shape whirling desperately beneath the ice, searching for a way out. Then Forollkin spotted a network of fine cracks spreading across the ice and hurried his companions to the safety of the further passage. Kerish lingered for a moment, half hoping and half dreading that the white shape would break through the surface.

"Is it the ice or your wits melting?" called back Gidjabolgo.

Kerish jumped as if he had been slapped and ran after the others.

Ten minutes' fast walking brought the travellers to a third courtyard which contained nothing but three tall statues in dull grey stone. The statues seemed to be unfinished. The hands were not divided into fingers and the faces had no eyes. Kerish was gripped by the idea that there were living creatures trapped inside the half-carved stone and that the unknown sculptor had stopped work because he was afraid of freeing them. Forollkin stepped confidently into the courtyard and three blind heads turned towards him.

The young Galkian moved back twice as fast but the nearest statue took one slow step after him. It stretched out its fingerless hands, moving them from side to side as if it was feeling its way. Then, in the far distance, a silver bell sounded the hour. With a grinding of stone, the statue turned and bowed. The other figures bowed ponderously back and they began a clumsy dance.

"Now!" whispered Kerish. He grabbed Gwerath's arm and ran with her across the courtyard, dodging past the stone figures, who seemed too absorbed in their dance to notice them. Forollkin and Gidjabolgo followed and they reached the passage just as the bell stopped ringing. On the last chime the statues bowed to each other and then three blind heads turned towards the travellers again.

Gidjabolgo broke into a trot and the others soon overtook him. Forollkin led them, taking right or left turns at random, alert for the first sound of slow, inexorable footsteps behind them, but he heard nothing except the ever present whispering. Round a bend in the passage they suddenly came on a fourth courtyard. Gidjabolgo leaned against a wall, getting his breath back, while the others stared into the silent courtyard.

It was paved with alternating slabs of black and crimson and on each of the black squares lay a huge, glittering jewel. The courtyard seemed innocent enough but the travellers were wary now.

"I'll go first," said Kerish and this time Forollkin didn't argue.

As the Prince stepped onto the first of the red squares, the jewel on the black slab beside it burst into a pillar of blue flame. He flinched away, not from heat but from an intense cold and the shower of blue sparks that fell on his clothes and skin were like slivers of ice.

"Come back!" shouted Forollkin but Kerish was already stepping diagonally onto the next red slab. The jewels lying on the black slabs to either side of it flared up and blue flames licked at the edge of his cloak. He twitched it on to the red square, but the hem of the cloak was already heavy with ice. He stooped to snap off the frozen silk, rubbed some warmth into his numbed fingers and called back to the others.

"I think it's safe if you keep to the red squares."

He moved diagonally across the courtyard, lighting the blue flames at every step, and the others followed cautiously. Gwerath came first, treading delicately; Gidjabolgo next, still breathing heavily; and Forollkin last, checking his long stride to keep within the red squares. By the time they reached the passage they were all shivering with cold but as Forollkin stepped off the last red slab the blue flames flickered, sank down and disappeared. The jewels lay glimmering innocently again on the smooth black squares. As they walked on, Kerish tried not to think about what

15

would have happened to him if he'd trodden first on black stone and tried to pick up a jewel.

After a few minutes, the travellers began to notice a gentle breeze blowing through the maze and Kerish thought he heard birdsong amongst the rustles and whispers. They took a left turn and were suddenly confronted by a fifth courtyard. Larger than the others, it was paved and walled in a warm golden stone and appeared to be quite empty. Forollkin moved hesitantly forward and then stopped so suddenly that Gwerath bumped into him.

"What is it?"

Forollkin held out his hand to show her a long thin scratch.

"I touched something sharp, but there's nothing there."

He swept his hand through the air and grunted in surprise and pain as more scratches appeared.

"Zeldin's Footsteps, whatever it is, it tears like thorns!"

The breeze ruffled Gwerath's hair and she suddenly began to twist and turn her head.

"Something's caught hold of my hair!"

Kerish reached up, his sensitive fingers apparently pressing thin air.

"What's happening?" demanded Gidjabolgo.

"It feels like the branch of a tree . . . "

Kerish closed his eyes and concentrated hard. Leaves brushed his cheek and all the birds of summer were singing nearby. The courtyard was filled by a neglected garden, choked with weeds and thorns.

"Draw your sword, Forollkin; we have to hack our way through a garden."

Kerish untangled Gwerath's hair from the bough of a fruit tree and they moved forward. Forollkin used his sword like a scythe to clear a path through the tangled undergrowth, but their progress was slow and painful. Invisible brambles sprang at the travellers, roots tripped them up and thorns snagged their clothes and skin. Kerish continually described the obstacles ahead of them, from low-hanging branches to piles of rotting fruit, black with insects, but he could not see his companions and the garden

16

at the same time and he often misjudged their position. Forollkin swore as he drove the edge of his blade into a tree trunk and Kerish opened his eyes.

"I'm sorry, I thought you were a bit further to the left."

Forollkin felt for the invisible tree trunk, thrust a knee against it and pulled out his sword. Kerish closed his eyes again and tried to find a path through a thicket of thorn bushes.

In another ten minutes the travellers had reached the genuine emptiness of the further passage and stood sucking their scratches or pulling burrs and thorns from their clothing. Kerish's eyes were still closed.

"It must have been a beautiful garden once . . . "

"If you say so," began Forollkin, "but it didn't feel beautiful. Come on." He strode off down the passage and the others followed. Round the very next corner they came on a sixth courtyard, far larger than the rest and divided by a wide crack in the crimson floor. Forollkin walked to the edge of the crack and looked down. He could see no bottom to the chasm but he heard a noise like the rushing of water very far below.

"Thank Imarko, there's a bridge," he said.

The bridge was a slender arch of polished stone with no kind of wall or handrail to make it easier to cross.

"I'll go first," ordered Forollkin, "then you, Gwerath, then Kerish and Gidjabolgo last. Don't look down, keep your eyes on the other side and walk slowly."

Forollkin stepped onto the slippery arch and Gwerath followed, her arms spread wide to help her balance. Gidjabolgo hesitated and Kerish felt a sudden reluctance to touch the bridge. He closed his eyes to concentrate on calmness, but what he saw in his mind's eye made him grab Gidjabolgo and shout a warning.

"Forollkin, run!"

The stone bridge was an illusion. The chasm was spanned by a frail arch of black ice and it was already cracking under the double weight.

"Gwerath, jump!"

Obeying the terror in Kerish's voice, Forollkin turned, grabbed Gwerath's wrist and leapt for the far side as the ice

17

splintered beneath their feet. The bridge snapped and chunks of ice fell into the chasm, shattering against its walls. For a long moment Gwerath struggled to regain her balance, one foot on solid stone, the other dangling above the chasm. Then Forollkin dropped to his knees, wrenching Gwerath towards him and they sprawled together on the crimson stone.

Kerish shouted across the courtyard.

"Are you both all right?"

Forollkin sat up. "I am, but, Gwerath, I must have hurt your wrist."

"It only hurts a little," whispered Gwerath, but her left wrist was already swelling and when Forollkin gently tried to feel the damage, she gasped with pain. He began to bandage it with his sash as Kerish paced along the edge of the chasm, looking for another way across.

"There was a fork in that last passage," said Gidjabolgo. "If we took it we might find a path to lead us round this courtyard."

Kerish agreed. "We'll have to try it. Forollkin, stay there and shout every so often so that we can judge how close we are. If we haven't reached you within an hour, go on and try to find the centre of the maze."

Forollkin nodded uneasily and watched Kerish and Gidjabolgo disappear back down the passage. He strained to follow the sound of their footsteps but the rustles and whispers that filled the maze were growing louder. He had the uncomfortable feeling that if he listened hard enough he would begin to understand what the whisperers were saying. Determined not to try, he turned back to Gwerath.

The left fork in the passage brought Kerish and Gidjabolgo to another courtyard, fractured by the same broad chasm. This time, instead of a bridge, the chasm was spanned by a convoluted stair of crimson stone that soared up to a great height before spiralling down again. Kerish stared at it warily.

"I see an empty staircase. No-one seems to be on it but . . . " said Gidjabolgo.

Kerish finished the sentence for him. "But you can hear them."

18

Forollkin called out from somewhere close but he was barely audible above the perpetual whispering and the sound of heavy footsteps. Kerish folded his hands over the Jewel of Zeldin and closed his eyes.

Two tall figures holding axes marched up the blood-red steps; a man with four arms crept downwards weeping; a naked child fled from a serpent and a one-legged bird hopped from step to step, pecking at its own breast. Kerish opened his eyes again but, to his horror, he could still see the creatures of the stair.

"Gidjabolgo, do you really see nothing on the stairs?"

"Nothing," repeated the Forgite.

"Then . . . I must guide you because the stairs are not empty. Take my arm and tread exactly where I tell you."

A figure slid towards them carrying a bunch of purple flowers with snakes for stems. It was a dazzle of jewels and silks held together by white sticks that parodied human bones. Kerish looked away from its face.

"Gidjabolgo, we may not . . . listen, if I've treated you unkindly in the past, I'm sorry. I . . ."

"Save your sorrow for yourself," snapped the Forgite and gripped the Prince's arm. Holding the Jewel of Zeldin to his heart, Kerish set foot on the lowest step of the crimson stair.

Gwerath sat cradling her aching wrist while Forollkin walked up and down the edge of the chasm. After a few minutes she said in a low voice, "I know you're still angry with me for following you into the Red Waste, but . . ."

"I'm not angry with you." Forollkin swung back towards her. "I'm angry with myself."

"Yourself! But why?"

Forollkin sat down beside her.

"I shouldn't have spoken to Kerish the way I did but I couldn't bear to be challenged by him then, just when I knew that I wasn't leading you well enough because of my fear of Saroc and his sorcery."

"You are not afraid," protested Gwerath, "you are never afraid."

"You don't know me, little cousin," Forollkin smiled wryly. "I am afraid of what I do not understand . . . I don't mind the odds against me being high, but I do mind not knowing what they are, and I wish to Zeldin that we hadn't dragged you into this danger too."

"I wanted to come." Gwerath plucked at the sash around her wrist. "It was my choice."

"Yes, but to leave your family, your home . . ."

"I was sorry to leave Eamey," murmured Gwerath, looking down at her lap. "I am sorry that the goddess has left me but I will never be sorry that I came away with you."

"But you don't always seem happy with us." Forollkin wished he could see her expression. "Gwerath, I've sometimes thought . . ."

He broke off as the rushing noise in the depths of the chasm grew suddenly louder.

"Oh, be careful . . ."

Ignoring Gwerath's warning, Forollkin lay flat on the crimson stone, gripped the edge of the chasm and looked down.

"There's something bright down there; bright and huge and it's coming up!"

Forollkin rolled away from the edge and stood up.

"We'd better take the passage and . . ."

He stopped as he saw what Gwerath was already staring at. Filling the passage was the cloud, a billowing mass of white, speckled with gold. Forollkin pulled Gwerath to her feet, drew his sword and spun round to face the chasm. From out of the blackness rose a second cloud of dazzling, shifting colours. After a few moments, he realized that this cloud was made up of hundreds of tiny gem-like birds furiously beating their wings. He ducked as scores of them flew over their heads and towards the passage.

Most of the birds rose up towards the red sky, but a few flew blindly into the path of the cloud. As they entered the swirling whiteness, golden particles rushed towards them. For a moment they still flapped their wings, struggling to fly upwards, then each hung motionless, stiff with gold. Forollkin and Gwerath backed towards the edge of the chasm as the cloud spread out until it filled the whole courtyard and began to roll towards them. Forollkin called out once, but only the whisperers answered him.

Kerish stood at the apex of the stair and without Gidjabolgo's support he would have fallen. The Forgite heard the heavy footsteps and a faint rasping, but Kerish could see what made the sounds and desperately wished that he couldn't. From one direction came the axe-bearers and from the other a man without hands or feet heaved himself painfully from step to step. So far the travellers had avoided touching any of the creatures but here the stairs were dangerously narrow.

"Down," ordered Kerish.

The echoing tread of the axe-bearers followed them down as Kerish picked his way carefully, holding up his cloak. There were pools of blood and scattered shards of bone on every third step. Gidjabolgo copied the Prince's movements and obeyed at once when ordered to stand still.

"It's nearly on us now!"

The Forgite could hear the panic that Kerish was barely suppressing.

"Back, back!" He pulled Gidjabolgo to the edge of the stair and the brink of the chasm as something moaned softly just a few inches away from them. Then Kerish was running down the stair again, dragging Gidjabolgo after him.

"Jump over the next two steps!" shouted Kerish.

Gidjabolgo didn't ask him why; he could hear an ominous hissing. The stair twisted into a spiral, which was far worse because Kerish could only guess at what might be round the next curve but he hurried on, because the axe-bearers were still close behind and he knew now what was in the sacks they carried.

Gidjabolgo gasped for breath, trying to keep up with the Prince, but suddenly Kerish stopped and clung to the stair pillar, his eyes dilated with horror. As he came level with Kerish, Gidjabolgo flinched from a fierce heat and the stench of burning flesh.

"It's alive!" Kerish was whispering. "It's still alive!"

Gidjabolgo shook him by the shoulders.

"Go on, we're nearly across."

Kerish forced himself to let go of the pillar and edged

down the stair. He stepped over the body of a woman, whose long white hair flowed across the crimson stone and down into the chasm, and then glanced back. The axe-bearers were closer than ever and one of them was taking off his mask. Kerish ran, ducking as the one-legged bird took off with a shriek of mocking laughter. Almost at once he stopped again and Gidjabolgo crashed into him.

"What is it?"

"The serpent," said Kerish.

It was coiled across three steps, in the act of devouring a struggling child. The serpent swallowed its prey and swayed to and fro, its long tongue flickering. Kerish stood petrified by its cruel gaze, then he heard a peal of laughter. A few steps above them stood another naked child, golden haired and beautiful like the first. The serpent hissed; the child ran. The hideous bulk began to uncoil as the serpent slithered upwards.

"Jump, Gidjabolgo!" called Kerish, as he leapt to the safety of the courtyard. Less agile than the Prince, Gidjabolgo felt the serpent brush against his cloak as he made his clumsy jump. The cloth turned green and began to rot away. He stared at it for a moment but then the Prince grabbed his hand and they ran for the passage.

When they were a long way from the stair, Kerish leaned against a cool crimson wall, his whole body trembling.

"Zeldin spare me from such sights and Imarko take them from my memory!"

"Would you have her take away a part of yourself?" asked the Forgite softly.

Kerish turned to face him.

"I couldn't have crossed that stair without you."

"We'd better take the right fork here," answered Gidjabolgo, "if we're to find our lost chicks."

Kerish nodded and they walked on. Every few minutes the Prince called out his brother's name but there was never any answer. They finally found their way back to the courtyard of the broken bridge, but except for a few bright feathers and a scattering of golden dust it was quite empty.

"Zeldin knows how long we were on that stair." Kerish glanced up at the red sun. By his reckoning it should have

22

set long ago but it still hung banefully in the cloudless sky. "They must have gone on."

Gidjabolgo looked unconvinced but said nothing and they headed back towards the heart of the maze. Kerish called to Forollkin again and again but his voice vanished into an eerie silence. The whispers and the rustlings were dying down and he almost missed them. He let Gidjabolgo go ahead of him and choose right or left turns at random but there seemed to be no more courtyards to cross. As they rounded a corner darkness fell, sudden and complete. Kerish stretched out his hands and found Gidjabolgo standing close to him.

"Now what do we . . . " began the Forgite, when the darkness lifted as suddenly as it had fallen. The red sun had been replaced by a leaden moon and a wave of pallid light broke across the maze.

Peering ahead Kerish saw that the passage seemed to be blocked by some kind of silvery foliage. At the cost of a few more scratches they squeezed through into a second garden. Against alabaster walls and between slabs of creamy marble grew pale-leaved, white-flowered shrubs and trees. Thorn bushes were patches of darkness and weeds sprang up through cracks in the paving, but the garden was still beautiful. Kerish walked towards a weeping tree heavy with scented blossom and trod on something sharp. He stooped to pick it up and saw that he was holding a silver butterfly with brightly enamelled wings. He guessed that it must once have flown but the mechanism was broken and there were cracks in the crimson enamel. Gidjabolgo had wandered ahead and Kerish hurried to catch him up. They came together to the heart of the garden, a shallow pool beneath a dead tree. The pool was choked with weeds but one patch of clear water reflected the melancholy face of Saroc.

Chapter 2

The Book of the Emperors: *Sorrows*
But he said to the mourners: "They that feed upon their grief
grow bloated with sorrow and cease to care if the world suffers
with them. Remember always that it is the duty of mankind to
be joyful and that it is a wise man who knows whether he
weeps for another or for himself."

KERISH and Gidjabolgo came slowly forward but Saroc did not look up until their reflections took shape beside his in the stagnant pool. They could see that he had once been strikingly handsome but now his appearance was as neglected as his garden.

"My Lord," began Kerish, but the sorcerer interrupted him.

"What are you holding in your hand?"

Startled, Kerish held out the broken butterfly.

"A child's toy, I think."

Saroc took it from the Prince. "I gave it to her here, on that last evening, because she had grown tired of this white and silver garden and longed for colour. I had made two gardens for my daughter, one for night and one for day. Pergon of Lamoth found her in the Day Garden and I swore that no-one should see it again, yet you saw . . . You are the first to ever reach the heart of my maze. Even Pergon did not cross the Red Stair."

"Your citadel is well guarded," said Kerish, "and your maze is filled with horrors."

"Horrors? Are there no dark places in your mind, Prince of the Godborn? Am I to blame if fools dash out their lives against my walls? May I not defend my solitude?" asked Saroc. "And what have you come to take from me? I have no second daughter."

"I think you know which treasure I have come for," said Kerish.

"I have no treasures," replied Saroc, "but you deserve some reward for your courage. I will grant each one of you one wish."

Kerish bowed.

"Thank you, Lord Saroc, and will you also answer one question?"

"Your companions are caught in my gold cloud," said Saroc, as if the question had already been asked. "They will glitter there until the Great Ocean sweeps over Seld unless you spend your wish on freeing them. Ah, I see this treasure means much to you. Are your companions' lives worth less? And you, Forgite, can I guess your desire too?"

Saroc turned his green gaze on Gidjabolgo and a twisted smile made his face look even sadder.

"A tawdry wish. I see that men have not grown wiser since I withdrew from the world and their dreams are still narrow; but I will grant your wish, on one condition."

"What condition?" asked Gidjabolgo warily.

"Come closer and I will whisper it to you."

Gidjabolgo knelt beside the sorcerer, his face almost touching Saroc's red hair. Kerish could not hear what was said, but he saw the Forgite's shallow eyes flood with revulsion.

"No!"

"No? But why not? What is he to you?"

From the sleeve of his robe Saroc drew out a crystal rod streaked with crimson.

"I will make it easy for you. There is no risk."

Gidjabolgo stood up. "Name some other condition."

Saroc leaned back against the dead tree. "Then name another wish."

Kerish willed the Forgite to ask for the release of Forollkin and Gwerath, but after a moment's thought, Gidjabolgo stooped to whisper something.

"There is only one being with the power to make such a wish come true," said Saroc in a gentler voice, "and that is yourself. Now, Prince, what is your choice?"

As he spoke, the white cloud crept into the Night Garden

25

and Kerish could just see two stiff golden figures trapped inside it.

"Set them free," he said quietly.

Saroc got up from beside the pool and touched the edge of the cloud with his crystal wand. The whiteness gradually dissolved away, leaving a flock of golden birds burnishing the air and the gleaming figures of Gwerath and Forollkin. Gold coated their skin and hair and clothes. Their eyes were closed and they no longer seemed to breathe. Saroc struck at them with his wand and cracks appeared and the gold began to flake away and drift to the ground. Then the sorcerer pointed the crystal wand at the birds and the air was filled with life and colour again, just as Forollkin sneezed and opened his eyes and Gwerath shook clouds of gold dust from her silver hair.

"Kerish, what . . . where . . . ?"

Forollkin blinked and sneezed again as Kerish ran up to him.

"It's all right, Forollkin. We've reached the centre of the maze and we're all safe."

"Quite safe," murmured Saroc. "Now leave my citadel."

For the first time, Gwerath and Forollkin noticed the tall, red-haired man, clutching his shabby cloak about himself as if he was cold.

"Go back the way you came," he was saying. "Nothing will harm you when you walk under my protection."

"Lord Saroc," began Kerish, "my companions will be grateful for your safe conduct, but I cannot leave until I have what I came for."

Saroc turned his back on the travellers and stared towards a gate in the white walls and the crimson tower beyond it.

"Ask nothing else of me and leave quickly while my gentle mood lasts. I do not want to hurt you, Prince, since you buried my poor, faithful Acanoth beside the cat you loved. Do you know how many of my creatures Pergon of Lamoth killed? My daughter laughed as she stepped over the bodies of the beasts she had played with day after day. Their only purpose was to guard her. I had to guard her. Only within my citadel and lands could I keep age and death away from her but all she wanted was to see Zindar. The little worlds I made for her were not enough. When Pergon told her that I kept her imprisoned out of jealousy, she believed him and went with him willingly. I had warned her again and again what would happen if she left my realm, but she thought it was a trick to stop her escaping from me. I was too late to save my daughter and I suppose in Seld they say that I killed her."

"Yes," said Kerish gently, "and they have learned to fear you."

"Then they are wiser than you, Prince of the Godborn. Leave Tir-Tonar!"

"Not until I have delivered my message from your wife."

The crystal wand snapped in Saroc's hands and three drops of crimson stained the marble paving.

"You mock me."

"No, Lord Saroc, we have come across the plains of Erandachu from Tir-Zulmar."

Saroc turned slowly and Kerish flinched at the anger in his face.

"If you don't believe us," said Forollkin hastily, "look at Gwerath here. You can see that she comes from Erandachu, from the shadow of the mountains. We have been there and we have seen your lady."

"Do you think I don't recognize one of my wife's worshippers?" asked Saroc "And the silver hair she gives them to mirror her own. Do the reflections still feed her vanity? Does she still revel in playing the goddess to the barbarians at her feet? Does she . . . "

"Lord Saroc!"

The urgent appeal in Kerish's voice made even the sorcerer pause. Gwerath was staring blankly at the Lord of Tir-Tonar and Kerish hoped she hadn't understood.

"My Lord, will you hear my message from Sendaaka?"

"She swore that she would never speak to me again."

"Centuries have passed since then, she has changed."

"Changed . . . how has she changed? No, don't tell me here. We must talk alone. You . . . " Saroc pointed his broken wand at Forollkin, Gwerath and Gidjabolgo. "Stay in this garden and you will be safe. Prince, come with me."

Gwerath watched Kerish and the sorcerer leave the garden and enter the crimson tower together, then she turned on Forollkin.

"What did he mean, that I worshipped his wife?"

Wishing that Kerish was there to answer for him, Forollkin said hesitantly, "Sendaaka was human once, but now she is immortal and . . ."

Gidjabolgo's harsh voice broke in.

"Your Goddess has quarrelled with her husband and sulks amongst the snows."

"Gidjabolgo!"

Forollkin's hand was on his sword hilt but Gwerath shouted, "No, let him tell me. I want to hear."

"Your Mountain Goddess is the Sorceress of Tir-Zulmar," said the Forgite. "As Saroc said, she chose to play the goddess and to force light into the darkness of the Erandachi."

"And you have seen her?"

"Seen her, touched her, spoken to her," declared Gidjabolgo. "In the citadel where she waits for her husband to humble himself to her."

"Gwerath, Sendaaka loves your people," said Forollkin anxiously. "Surely it doesn't matter that she isn't what you thought? Everything that she gave to the Children of the Wind was good."

"She gave us lies," whispered Gwerath.

"No more than any other deity, but if our Prince gets his way, Sendaaka's reign will soon be over. She will abandon her people," said Gidjabolgo, "and follow her lover to Seld and she is the image in which you are made."

"Thank you, Gidjabolgo," murmured Gwerath, "I see now."

She covered her face with her hands. "Oh, how you must have laughed at us."

"No, Gwerath, truly we didn't!"

Forollkin tried to put his arms around her but she pushed him away.

"And Kerish . . . he pretended to serve the goddess, to be her Torgu and all the time he knew that she was false and was mocking the Sheyasa."

"No, Gwerath, we just thought that it was best not to . . ."

"Oh yes, Galkians would know what's best for the poor blind Sheyasa. No, don't touch me, leave me alone!"

Gwerath ran from them, struggling through thorn bushes, and crouched down against a white wall in the furthest corner of the garden. Forollkin could hear her sobbing, but when he moved to follow her, Gidjabolgo stood in his path, grinning like a deathshead.

"Don't be a fool. Let her spew out her misery alone or she'll link you with it. Leave her alone and with any luck she'll blame your brother."

"What could you understand about feelings?" asked Forollkin angrily, but he turned back.

Kerish and Saroc entered the lowest chamber in the tower. Lit by fire and candle-light, it was crowded with books, scrolls and curious instruments that Kerish could put no names to. After the terrors of the maze, the room seemed very ordinary and in the gentle light the haggard face of Saroc seemed calmer and more human. The sorcerer tossed down his cloak and wand and moved to sit by a southerly window, overlooking a part of the citadel that the travellers had not seen.

Kerish sat down on a soft rug beside the fire and stared up at the sea-birds, carved in pale stone, whose shimmering wings held up the roof of the chamber. For a time there was silence and Kerish was grateful for a moment's pause to think very carefully about what he was going to say to Saroc. The sorcerer sighed and said wearily, "Forgive me, Prince, I was always the worst of hosts, Sendaaka used to . . . You must be tired and hungry. There is food and wine on the table there."

Kerish shook his head.

"I couldn't touch anything now, but my brother and the others . . ."

"I had forgotten them," said Saroc simply, and there was silence again.

Kerish noticed old stains on the fur rug and dust on tables

and chairs carelessly piled with books and scrolls. At length, he timidly asked the purpose of a coloured sphere that hung in front of one of the windows.

"What? Oh, it's a kind of a map. Vethnar and I worked on it together. Look closer and you might recognize Galkis . . . but the Godborn are always more interested in looking up at the stars than in noticing what lies at their feet. What other people would be content never to know what lies beyond their eastern border?"

"Zeldin himself forbade us to go more than three days' journey east of Far-Tryfarn as a test of our loyalty," answered Kerish. "Who is Vethnar?"

"He is the Sorcerer of Tir-Melidon, the Lord of Silnarnin. The three of us used to study together, here in this room. What does Sendaaka say to me?"

Kerish flinched at the suddenness of the question and then recovered himself.

"She is lonely and still grieves, as you do, for your daughter. She asks you to give up your key and travel north to fetch her from Tir-Zulmar."

"Give up *my* key! Must I surrender everything? Must I suffer for her pride? What did she tell you about me and about our life together? I can see from your expression that she taught you to blame me."

Saroc leaned back against the window. The moonlight sliding over his face accentuated the hollows of his cheeks and the brilliance of his green eyes.

"It was Sendaaka who could not bear to be equalled. I would gladly have given up my key if she had been willing to do the same, but she cared more about the fame of her wisdom than my love!"

"I don't know whether that was true in the past," said Kerish, "but it certainly isn't now."

"And am I to abandon everything," demanded Saroc, "when at last Sendaaka crooks her little finger and says, 'Come to me, husband'?"

Kerish stood up. "The keys," he began slowly, "were they worth the price you paid for them? What did either of you gain?"

"Nothing," said Saroc bitterly. "Nothing but time

enough to realize that we had gained nothing. I am sick of night. We will have day again."

Unseen hands snuffed out the candles and doused the fire as sunlight poured in through the tall windows.

"So," continued Saroc, "you are saying to me that I must give up my key and die, while Sendaaka keeps her power and immortality."

"When you reach Tir-Zulmar, she will renounce her key."

"What proof do I have of that?" asked the sorcerer. "Perhaps all she wants is to avenge our daughter's death on me; perhaps she longs to have me mortal and helpless in cold Tir-Zulmar and to watch me die . . ."

Kerish's hands kept creeping to the keys at his waist, hidden beneath his tunic. Sendaaka's key was the answer to all Saroc's questions, but it was the one argument that the Prince was forbidden to use.

"I can offer you no proof of her intentions," said Kerish steadily, "I can only ask you to remember her as she was and make your own judgement."

"You said that she had changed. Is she still beautiful?"

"I had never seen such beauty before," answered Kerish. "She is like the sheen of frost on a winter morning."

"Frost kills," said Saroc. "Come here."

Kerish crossed to the window. Below lay a sunny courtyard, hedged with flowering trees. At a long table strewn with books and scrolls a woman sat reading. Her silver hair hid her face but he recognized the pale hands that turned the musty pages of her book. Saroc opened the window and called down to her. The woman looked up and she was as beautiful as Kerish had remembered, except that her eyes were empty of intelligence or feeling.

"See, my spells can summon up her beauty. What do I need with the reality?"

"Surely it was the reality that you loved!" protested Kerish. "Her mind, her feelings . . . not some beautiful, silent image. Think what you achieved when you were together, working as equals . . ."

Shrill laughter floated in through the open window. A girl with pale gold hair ran into the courtyard, followed by a

31

boy. He was red-haired like Saroc but his eyes were silvery-grey. The woman put down the book and smiled and they both kissed her cheek.

"Your daughter," murmured Kerish, "but the boy . . ."

"We never had a son," said Saroc. He clapped his hands and the smiling figures froze.

"I should not have accepted the key." Saroc closed the window. "But I was foolish enough to think that I knew what I wanted."

Kerish sat down on the stone sill beside the sorcerer.

"Perhaps life isn't bearable unless you think that."

"Is that what you have found, Prince? Isn't your quest for the keys enough for you?"

"I want the keys with all my heart," answered Kerish, "but I wish I knew that I was right to want them. When we set out I was quite certain about it; now I'm not."

"I cannot return lost certainties," said Saroc; "not even a sorcerer can do that."

"There is one thing that I am sure of, though," continued Kerish. "Surrendering your key and trusting Sendaaka is the only way out for you. In a sense Pergon of Lamoth was right, your daughter was a prisoner, but so are you."

For a moment Kerish thought that he had been too bold. Saroc was angry and his quest would end here. Then the sorcerer got up, strode across the room, opened a chest and drew out a golden casket.

"Take it then, take it, whether you bring me reprieve or execution. As if it mattered which . . ." Saroc took a deep breath and spoke more calmly. "Take the casket. You cannot open it without Sendaaka's key, but come north with me, and I will plead for you, if not for myself."

Kerish stood up again to accept the casket but he immediately put it down on a table and drew out the third key.

"Thank you, Lord Saroc, but there is no need. Sendaaka has already renounced her key."

Saroc stared at the white gem glittering in the golden haft.

"But you said . . ."

"Forgive me; Sendaaka ordered me not to tell you what she had done. She wanted one last test of your love."

"A test!"

Saroc's voice was thick with anger but then he began to laugh, suddenly looking very much younger.

"A test? How very like her; she can't have changed at all."

Kerish opened the casket and drew out a golden key, set with a crimson gem. Within a few seconds there were four keys dangling from the chain at his waist.

"Lord Saroc, will you help me a little further? I must find the next key."

The sorcerer nodded absently, his thoughts already racing north.

"Vethnar of Tir-Melidon holds the sixth key, but for the fifth you must journey to Tir-Roac, the heart of the Dead Kingdom. Shubeyash possesses the fifth key, or rather it possesses him. Since Roac died no-one has entered the citadel and returned."

"I must," said Kerish grimly.

Saroc touched the Jewel of Zeldin where it hung, half-hidden, in the folds of Kerish's tunic.

"Then this jewel will draw King Shubeyash to you but it may also prove your best defence."

"Elmandis said the same, but he wouldn't tell me why."

"Elmandis would make a secret of the time of day," said Saroc impatiently.

"Then will you tell me how to use the jewel?" asked Kerish.

"You cannot use it," answered Saroc, "but it may use you. I can tell you the legend of the Jewels of Zeldin, though you might find a different story in the *Book of Secrets*. It is said that your Foremother, Imarko, brought a mirror with her into Galkis; a precious mirror, not of metal but of glass. As she lay dying, Zeldin appeared to her, not in the human form he wears in Zindar but in all his empyreal glory. That glory was reflected in Imarko's mirror and it was broken by his radiance. Ever afterwards the shards retained his incandescent image and they were cut and worn as jewels

33

by the High Priests and Emperors of Galkis. Yours is the last remaining Jewel of Zeldin . . . no, don't take it off."

"I can't wear it now that I know. I can't!"

Kerish's fingers fumbled with the cirge chain.

"You must. It is your birthright," said Saroc sternly. "You cannot escape it. Wear it always."

"Only if I must," answered Kerish, and the jewel seemed to burn at his breast with a cold fire. "Tell me then, how should we enter Roac?"

"I cannot tell you. Go to the island of Gannoth and ask its ruler how to enter the Dead Kingdom. Gannoth is the guardian of Roac now."

"Thank you, Lord Saroc," murmured Kerish. "Thank you from all of Galkis."

"For so much thanks, perhaps I should give you one more thing," said the sorcerer. "One more warning. Though I did not know it at the time, I had to choose between the key to power and human love. Be very sure you understand the price that you will have to pay for freeing the Saviour of Galkis."

Shortly after the false dawn, food and wine were brought to the Night Garden, carefully carried by anxious-eyed vermillion beasts. Forollkin and Gidjabolgo were reluctant to touch the feast but the creatures whimpered and rubbed their foreheads in the dust and nibbled at the food to show that it was good. Gidjabolgo accepted a dish of curds from an outstretched paw and Gwerath emerged from behind the thorn bushes to wash her tear-swollen face in the pool. Forollkin could not think what to say to her and the strange meal was eaten in silence. When they had finished, the creatures took the empty dishes away with burbles of satisfaction. Gidjabolgo wandered round the garden sniffing the white flowers and Forollkin and Gwerath sat at opposite ends of the pool.

Forollkin finally cleared his throat to speak just as Saroc and Kerish walked together through the archway in the white wall. The sorcerer looked round the Night Garden as if he was seeing it with new eyes.

"It was beautiful once, Prince, but now the thorns are

thick as memories. I will destroy them and all my citadel before I leave. Then I will set you on your way for the court of Seld."

"Surely you won't destroy your creatures?"

It was Gwerath who spoke and Saroc studied her face for a moment before answering.

"No. They will live as long as I do. Princess, I had forgotten that you were hurt. Give me your hand."

He untied Forollkin's sash and encircled Gwerath's swollen wrist with his thumb and forefinger. She felt a few seconds of intense cold and then the pain was gone.

"Thank you," she said tonelessly and Kerish looked at her anxiously. He would have said something to her but Saroc spoke first.

"Come, you need not endure the maze again. We will take an easier path to the outer wall."

He stamped his foot and two paving stones slid back to reveal a descending stair. Saroc led the travellers down into a long straight tunnel, where polished walls gave back a thousand different reflections of Sendaaka's face. Walking quickly to keep up with the sorcerer's eager stride, Kerish answered only one of his brother's questions.

"Yes, he gave me the key. Ask me about it later. Not now."

It seemed to take no more than an hour to reach the outer wall. They passed through the crack in the ramparts, out onto the red sand and the travellers froze as the guardians swooped down on them, with high, excited screams. Dozens of the creatures landed close to Saroc and he walked amongst them, stroking each scaled head and speaking their names. They caught at his robe with their clawed hands, as if they were beseeching him to stay with them, but Saroc shook his head. He called out three times, and through the crack in the ramparts ran and loped and crawled the creatures of the maze. Grotesque or beautiful, they all crowded round the sorcerer, yelping and mewing, hissing and growling.

Forollkin kept his hand on his sword hilt as one of the stone dancers lumbered past and Kerish flinched as the denizens of the Red Stair left Tir-Roac, but none of the creatures took any notice of the travellers. Saroc touched and spoke to all the beasts of his maze and then ordered them to move away from the shadow of the walls. The travellers soon found themselves standing amongst the creatures from the courtyard of the stone flowers, watching the sorcerer.

Saroc raised his left hand and fire flowed from its fingers and seemed to burrow through the sand towards Tir-Tonar. As it reached the base of the walls it leapt into a great sheet of flame that encircled and engulfed the citadel. The travellers moved back, but they felt no heat and the flames burned silently. Gradually the crimson walls blackened, then glowed white and finally began to crumble. Within an hour there was nothing left but the Red Stair over the abyss.

Then he raised his right hand and pointed upwards. The sky began to lose its crimson glare and change to a soft blue. Kerish was the first to notice a small grey cloud forming and soon the sky was full of them. Saroc made a circle in the air and shafts of crimson pierced the clouds. Sheets of silvery rain fell and the air was filled with smoke from the smouldering ruins. Saroc pointed his right hand downwards. The travellers had to move quickly as a spring welled up beneath their feet. All around them, grass thrust its way through the red sands and plants grew and flowered within minutes. The creatures of the maze sniffed at them, suspiciously at first and then with pleasure. Some began to browse, others rolled over on their backs, rubbing the new scents into their bodies. All of the creatures began to drift away from the ruins of Tir-Tonar.

Saroc let his arms fall to his sides and he began to shiver beneath his sodden robe. The rain had untangled his long red hair and the brilliance of his eyes had been dowsed with the flames; now they were smokey grey and full of human warmth. He turned to the travellers.

"My way lies north, yours south. I will summon Sendaaka's horses to me, since you will not need them again. Lord Djezaney still waits to escort you to his Queen at Mel-Kellin."

Saroc looked around him. Close by, the stone figures had joined hands and danced in a circle, trampling the new flowers; and the golden child stroked the coils of the serpent as they lay down together beside a stream.

"The Red Waste shall be a garden again and a sanctuary for my creatures. Their monstrous strangeness will protect them from the cruelty of men and your Lilahnee will have a quiet grave."

Chapter 3

The Book of the Emperors: *Teachings*
*"You have been commanded to love one another, but I tell you
to understand one another and that is the harder task."*

WHEN the slow barge that Djezaney had comman-
deered for the last part of their journey finally
reached the capital, the travellers found that news of their
safety had gone before them and a royal welcome awaited
them. Four courtiers had carried Pellameera's ivory chair to
the water's edge and Lord Djan knelt beside it, stroking the
hem of the Queen's robe. Six grave ladies-in-waiting held a
silken canopy over the Queen's head but Forollkin looked
only at Pellameera. Green gems crowned her lustrous hair
and she was even more beautiful than he had remembered.

The crew of the barge jumped on to the bank, with
mooring spikes and ropes. Kerish offered Gwerath a hand
to help her ashore but the Princess of the Sheyasa had
overcome her initial distrust of the first boat she had ever
seen. Ignoring the Prince she leaped confidently on to the
turf, followed by Forollkin and Gidjabolgo. Kerish-lo-
Taan bowed to Pellameera and she gave him her hand to
kiss. "Dear Prince, we rejoice to see you safe. I hear
strange tales from the north that Tir-Tonar has fallen and
the sorcerer is dead."

"Saroc is not dead, your Majesty, but he has destroyed
Tir-Tonar and left your Queendom. The Red Waste will
become a garden again but it is full of the monstrous
creatures of the sorcerer and still too dangerous to enter."

"Unless you are as gallant as a Galkian." Pellameera
smiled as Forollkin bowed before her, and nodded
graciously to Gidjabolgo.

38

"You must tell me all about your adventures but where is Djezaney?" Resplendent in rose silk, the Seldian knelt before his Queen, sweeping off his feathered hat. "I must hear your story too."

"There is little to tell, your Majesty," said Djezaney sullenly. "Banished from beauty, I waited in the White Hills till flames roared through the Red Waste and my four charges returned."

"Four!" The Queen stared at Gwerath, from her shabby riding boots to the untidy braids of her silver hair. "You also had business with the sorcerer, Princess?"

"More than I knew," said Gwerath quietly.

"Djezaney was supposed to keep the Princess safe in camp," began Forollkin.

"She told me she would ride after her cousins," said the Seldian, "and I am not accustomed to disobeying royal ladies."

Pellameera smiled slightly but Djan murmured, "So you skulked in the White Hills while the Prince and his brother conquered Saroc."

"Is hiding beneath my skirts more honourable, Djan?" enquired Pellameera and she gave Lord Djezaney her hand. As he kissed each finger Forollkin suddenly stepped forward.

"Madam, I have brought you something from the Red Waste."

He slipped a crystal bracelet from his arm and knelt to offer it to Pellameera.

"Why it is the jewel I gave to Theligarn when our first daughter was born. How . . . ?"

"We found his body," said Forollkin grimly. "He was slaughtered by the guardians of Tir-Tonar."

"Your gift will bring back his memory," murmured Pellameera.

Forollkin wished he had never spoken but, after a moment, the Queen handed the bracelet to one of her ladies and, smiling brightly, she questioned Kerish.

"Tell me, where is your pretty marsh cat?"

"She died, your Majesty, fighting the guardians in the Red Waste."

"Ah, I am sorry you have lost so rare and valuable a creature. I must find another pet to please you. I cannot have you looking so sad now that your quest is accomplished."

"I want no other pet," Kerish answered, "and our quest is far from accomplished. We must sail to Gannoth to ask its King for help."

"To Gannoth? A Prince of Galkis is free to go where he chooses but I hope you will endure my poor hospitality for a few days longer. Perhaps your brother can persuade you."

She smiled at Forollkin.

"And you, Princess, so pale and haggard, you must rest."

There was little Kerish could do but accept. Horses, garlanded with summer flowers, were brought to the travellers for the short ride to the palace. Four noblemen lifted the Queen's chair and she beckoned to the Prince to ride beside her.

"I have news that may banish those sombre thoughts. The ship that brought the Emperor's Envoy is still in port."

"The *Zeloka*?"

"I believe that is the name. I will order the captain to wait on you. He has a letter for your Highness from Galkis."

"Thank you, but I would rather visit the *Zeloka* myself."

"An escort will be arranged for you. Are you fond of ships, Prince? You must come sailing with me in my new pleasure skiff . . ."

All the way to the palace Pellameera chattered lightly of the pleasures that she could offer her guests and Kerish filled the rare pauses with expressions of polite interest.

The Queen's palace and the mansions of her ladies were built on the south bank of the dark, swift-flowing Rellendon, while north-east, across the placid Mel, lay the poorer quarters of Mel-Kellin. Even there, the wooden shacks were brightly painted and the merchants' quarter on the north bank of the Rellendon was a blaze of colour. The walls of the palace were tiled in azure and rose, cream and gold while the Queens of Seld, with hard bright faces, stared out from eternal gardens. Above the wall Gwerath glimpsed the gigantic heads of birds, beasts and nodding flowers. Her hands tightened on the reins and it took her a few moments to realize that she was seeing the fantastic roofs of a circle of wooden castles.

Once inside the palace, the travellers were led through a formal garden, past a miniature lake to a wooden pavilion shaped like a fully open water flower. They were shown into a splendid suite of rooms, each tiled with patterns of fish and flowers in blue and green and white. For furnishings there were low tables and porcelain couches so fragile that Forollkin was afraid to sit down.

Food was discreetly brought in covered dishes and when they had eaten, four pages came to help the travellers to dress for an entertainment in their honour, to be held in the palace gardens. Kerish put on his best robe and his zeloka jewels but Forollkin merely changed into his other set of travelling clothes. Gigjabolgo curled up in a corner with a pile of books that had been put out for their amusement.

"If my masters can bear my absence, I'm sure Queen Pellameera will not notice it . . ."

When Kerish was ready he tapped on Gwerath's door. Pellameera had sent gifts of clothing but Gwerath had dismissed the pages who had brought them and the lovely dresses lay crumpled on the floor. Kerish heard a muffled answer to his knock and walked into the room. Gwerath was kneeling in the window seat, her face pressed against a pane of glass. Below, a boat load of musicians was being launched on to the lake and pages were climbing trees to hang up coloured lanterns.

"Aren't you coming down?" asked Kerish.

"I told them my head hurt," mumbled Gwerath.

"And does it?"

Surprised, Gwerath looked round.

"Oh I don't blame you," said Kerish as he crossed the tiled floor. "I'd get out of it too if I could."

Gwerath blinked at the dazzle of his jewelled collar.

"I thought you admired the Queen."

"No. Though I am beginning to feel sorry for her." He sat down beside her on the window seat.

"Well, Forollkin admires her," said Gwerath hesitantly.

Kerish looked down at the servants scurrying across the

41

lawn with piles of cushions.

"He admires her and he hates her. He just likes you. Which would you prefer?"

"Does he really like me?"

It was the first time that Kerish had seen a glimmer of her old eagerness in Gwerath's face since they had left Tir-Tonar. During their dull journey to Mel-Kellin she had been sullen and withdrawn. "If you like a woman who talks, she talks well," Tayeb had said; but his daughter was no longer the lively inquistive Torga of the Goddess and Kerish was afraid for her. Forollkin kept saying that Gwerath would get over it if they left her alone but Kerish saw that she was closing herself off from them and from everything. He desperately wanted to be the one to stop her, but he knew that Forollkin's name was the key.

"Oh, Forollkin likes most people," said Kerish cruelly. "Are you sure you won't come down?"

"I'll watch from here," answered Gwerath and she pressed her face against the cool glass again.

Pages escorted the two Galkians to a dais set up in the formal garden. Seated beside the Queen they were entertained by displays of traditional Seldian dances. Lord Djan excelled in a dance that involved juggling with fans and knives, while Lord Djezaney, his clothes jangling with silver bells, led a troupe of noblemen in a dance that was meant to imitate a rainstorm.

Forollkin furtively watched Pellameera, fastening in his memory the strand of copper hair that fell across her soft cheek, the folds of white silk at her slender waist, the long, dark lashes that hid the lambent green of her eyes. Kerish spent a tedious evening courteously foiling the Queen's persistent questions about the nature of his quest. Both the Galkians were glad when midnight released them.

They slept late the next morning and it was not until noon that the two brothers were ready to leave for the harbour to visit the *Zeloka*.

"Forollkin. . ." Kerish pulled on one of his gloves. "See if you can coax Gwerath to come with us."

"That's a good idea, she ought to see a real ship."

As he left, Gidjabolgo muttered, "We have a saying in Forgin — 'Every new love brings a new hate into being.' Thank you for providing me with fresh amusement."

Kerish pulled on his other glove before he answered, "I shall do my best to disappoint you, Gidjabolgo."

Gwerath agreed to come, so she and the two Galkians rode borrowed horses towards the main harbour, flanked by an escort of Seldian soldiers. Their route took them past the high garden walls of the great mansions, through the quietest part of the city. Quiet, at least, in the noonday heat, when most Seldians were sleeping or taking meals in the privacy of inner rooms but everywhere there was evidence of a restless passion for change. Many buildings were being altered to fit new and ever more fantastical fashions. Workmen and craftswomen dozed amongst the heaps of broken tiles and discarded statues at each street-corner, while scaffolding surrounded half-demolished towers and the wooden skeletons of extravagant, sometimes dangerously frail mansions.

Kerish and Forollkin hardly noticed the city; they were looking ahead, eager for their first glimpse of the *Zeloka*. At last, they rounded a corner and saw the Galkian ship, ablaze with purple and gold, rocking on the dark waters of the Rellendon. Kerish stared at it as if he could hardly believe that it was real and Gwerath's face filled with wonder. Forollkin smiled at her involuntary tribute to the stately beauty of the jewel of the Galkian fleet and swung her down from her tall horse.

They were escorted aboard to receive a joyful welcome from Captain Engis, who hurried to kiss the Prince's hand and salute Forollkin.

"Your Highness, my Lord . . . I never thought I'd see you again. I cursed myself for trusting any Frian. No-one could give me any news of you and I feared . . ."

"Zeldin was with us," said Kerish. "Gwerath, may I present Engis, Captain of the *Zeloka*. Captain, this lady is my cousin, the Princess of the Sheyasa."

Armed with a dagger and dressed in shabby boy's clothing, Gwerath looked nothing like Engis's idea of a princess but he knelt and stammered a welcome. Forollkin quickly suggested that they all go below to talk and, when the Prince had persuaded the rest of the crew to stop prostrating themselves before him, Engis led the travellers to his cabin and sent for the best Galkian wine. Kerish and Forollkin drank it with delight but Gwerath took one sip and wrinkled her nose at its dryness.

"Now, Captain," Kerish leaned back in his chair to look up at the Galkian symbols carved on the beams; the starflower and the winged circle, the silver horse and the horned moon of Imarko. "Now, Captain, we should be glad of any news from Galkis."

"I'll tell your Highness all I know."

"And all that you conjecture," added Forollkin.

"Ah, I'm no courtier," said Engis "and a man must be more careful of his tongue now that the Emperor Ka-Litraan, may his soul rejoice with Zeldin, is dead."

"When he announced his death, did he seem ill?" asked Kerish. "Or in pain?"

"I spoke to the Envoy who had been at the ceremony, your Highness, and he said that the Emperor had seemed well and strong and very calm. Yet afterwards his Majesty refused to go to the Chamber of Darkness. He waited for his end somewhere deep in the gardens of the Inner Palace." Engis lowered his voice. "It's even rumoured that he wanted to be buried there."

"Rimoka would never have allowed him that," murmured Kerish.

"And the coronation," began Forollkin, "that should have taken place by now."

"Yes, my Lord," agreed Engis, "when I left Ephaan, the Crown Prince had already begun his journey to Hildimarn, to be crowned by the High Priestess and Prince Im-lo-Torim."

"By Im-lo-Torim!" said Forollkin sharply, "but the High Priest . . ."

"Our good Lord Izeldon has been very ill these six months or more," answered Engis. "Perhaps by now our Lady Imarko has led him through the dark."

"No," whispered Kerish, "I would have felt him go."

Engis felt his skin prickle as he looked into the eyes of the Godborn. "Yes, your Highness."

"And my sister, Ka-Metranee," said the Prince. "How is she?"

"The High Priestess has not left the sanctuary of our Lady's temple for more than a year now," began Engis cautiously, "and there are rumours . . ."

"That she is mad?" asked Forollkin bluntly.

"Oh no, my Lord; only that she weeps day and night and speaks of nothing but darkness and defeat."

To fill the silence Engis poured out more wine.

"There is one more piece of news, your Highness . . . just after the Emperor announced his death, he pardoned the Princess Zyrindella. She is no longer a prisoner in her own palace."

"The Empress must have been furious!" said Forollkin, astonished.

"I would not know, my Lord," Engis studied the table, "but the impious do say that the late Emperor wished to anger her with his last breath."

"I can well believe it," said Forollkin.

"It is the custom of the Godborn to forgive their enemies before death," murmured Kerish.

"Why ever he did it, I wish he hadn't," said Forollkin. "Now, Engis, tell me about the border situation. Are the Brigands of Fangmere still troublesome?"

"On land, no," answered Engis, "but the Sea of Az is thick with their ships."

"And the southern border?"

The Captain shrugged.

"Lord Jerenac does what he can, but he has been pushed back to the banks of the Jenze by the Khan of Orze and they say that a great army is gathering against us in Oraz."

Forollkin and Kerish asked many questions while Gwerath sat forgotten and bewildered by the names of unknown people and places. All she understood was that the news was bad.

"But as to news from the Inner Palace," Engis was saying, "this letter should tell you more."

He handed the Prince a roll of parchment, tied with a green ribbon and bearing Kelinda's seal.

"This was entrusted to me by Queen Kelinda herself, in

45

case I should find your Highness again."

"Is there much speculation in Galkis about our journey?"

"Yes, your Highness. It's generally known now that you sailed to Lan-Pin-Fria and we all feared that you had died in the marshes. To be truthful there were some who . . ."

"Who hoped we had? Don't look so anguished; it isn't a surprise."

"I thought I should warn your Highness, if you're sailing back to Galkis now . . ."

"We're not going home," said Kerish tersely and he broke the seal on the parchment.

"Oh, my Lord, I'd forgotten, there's a letter for you too, from your mother." Engis opened his chest to search for it.

"I thought your mother was dead," said Gwerath. "You never talk about her."

Forollkin took the letter and read it, frowning deeply.

The Captain nervously offered Gwerath more wine but she slid her hand over her cup and shook her head.

"Kelinda is well," said Kerish, looking up from his letter. "She doesn't complain but obviously our brother treats her no better than before . . ." He suddenly remembered Engis's presence and asked, "Where do you sail to now?"

"To Gannoth, your Highness, to take the Royal Envoy to the coronation of its new King. Then I have to take Queen Pellameera's letters of congratulation back to the new Emperor and Empress and to Queen Kelinda."

"I think we may trouble you for a passage to Gannoth. How soon do you leave?"

"I would sail as soon as you ordered it but there is a chain across the Mouth of the Rellendon that is only lifted by the Queen's command."

"Then we must be courteous to the Queen of Seld for a little longer," said Kerish.

As they rode through streets that were still almost deserted, Gwerath was full of questions.

"Why did your father hate his Empress and who is Zyrindella and what did he forgive her for?"

"Zyrindella is our father's daughter by the wife of the Governor of Tryfania," answered Kerish. "She is married

46

to our cousin, Prince Li-Kroch, who is not quite . . ."

"Who is mad," broke in Forollkin, "and she has a son, Kor-Li-Zynak, but not by Li-Kroch."

"Is that wrong?" asked Gwerath.

"Well, I . . . anyway," Forollkin hurried on, "Zyrindella has ambitions for her son. She is probably planning to put her son, or her husband, on the throne. She has two half-brothers, Zeenib and Yxin, the sons of the Governor of Tryfania and if they support her, Zyrindella could split off the northern provinces from our Empire."

Gwerath frowned.

"But your eldest brother is Emperor now. Won't he stop Zyrindella?"

"He is Emperor in name only; his mother, Rimoka, rules through him and he has no sons."

"Then who will be Emperor after him?" asked Gwerath.

"Im-lo-Torim, Rimoka's other son, is the Second Prince but once he becomes High Priest he can never be Emperor. That leaves Kerish and then Li-Kroch."

"But why not you?" demanded Gwerath. "You are older than Kerish."

"I am not a Prince," said Forollkin calmly. "The Emperor did not choose to marry my mother and go through the rites that would have made me inherit all the gifts of the Godborn."

"Among the Sheyasa," began Gwerath, "the strongest man becomes the Chieftain."

"It may soon be the same in Galkis," said Forollkin, with a grim smile. "Kerish, are you falling asleep in the saddle? Was the wine too much for you?"

As Kerish swayed in his saddle, he saw that his hands had become strangely distant and the hoofbeats stabbed through his head. His voice came out as a whisper.

"Something's wrong."

Forollkin leaned over to take the reins from his brother's limp hands and the first arrow hissed over his head.

By the time the unseen archer fired again, Forollkin had dragged Kerish out the saddle and behind his horse. The second arrrow thudded into a wall just above them. A third shot was impossible; the soldiers of the escort were already rushing towards a grille in a garden wall from which the arrows came. It took the soldiers a minute to kick open the only door in the wall and Forollkin guessed they'd have little chance of catching the archer if the man knew his way about the mansion he was shooting from.

Kerish picked up one of the green feathered arrows.

"Be careful, your Highness!" The Captain of the escort gingerly took the arrow and wrapped it in his cloak. "It may be poisoned."

The street was filling with workmen from nearby houses and curious faces were appearing at windows.

"Princess, your Highness, we must go on quickly," begged the Captain, "or rumour will fly round the city and the Queen . . ."

The travellers agreed to ride straight back to the palace and one of the soldiers was sent racing ahead to inform Pellameera of the attack on her guests.

The Queen acted swiftly and it was only three hours later that the Galkians were summoned to her private apartments to hear the results of her investigations. A page led them across a gilded bridge to an island in the centre of an artificial lake. A giant wooden bird, glazed with thousands of feather-patterned tiles in white and soft grey, dominated the island from a clump of carved reeds, cunningly painted, and each twice the height of a man. The page brought the Galkians through the stiff, silent reeds to a door in the breast of the hollow bird. Inside was a lavishly furnished chamber, lit by scented lamps, where the Queen entertained her most favoured courtiers. Kerish and Forollkin hardly had time to look at it before the page was asking them to climb the spiral stair hidden within the long curved neck of the bird. A hundred steps brought them to the Queen's bedchamber.

Pellameera was lying on a couch combing out her newly washed hair. As the evening sunlight streamed through the tinted windows, each hair was like a rainbow. The Galkians kissed her hand and were invited to sit down among the plump cushions on one of the window seats. Through the golden glass of the bird's right eye, they had a magnificent view of the twelve wooden castles that made up the palace. The other eye looked out over the river and the royal tombs at the water's edge.

"My dear Prince . . ." began Pellameera, "how can I express my anger, my distress at such an attempt on the lives of my guests in my own capital!"

"No shadow of blame falls across your Majesty," answered Kerish. "We imagine that the assassin was Galkian, or at least in Galkian pay."

Pellameera did not seem surprised.

"It may be so, though I grieve to say that three of my own ladies have been murdered in the past year by Seldian malcontents. The crew of the *Zeloka* have been thoroughly questioned. The Captain was on board at the time of the shooting but . . ."

"Captain Engis is above suspicion," said Kerish stiffly.

Pellameera teased out a tangle with her ivory comb.

"No-one is above suspicion, Prince. I wonder that you have survived so long without learning that. Three or four of the *Zeloka*'s crew were in the city at the time of the attack and could have fired the arrows. As they are not my subjects I could not have them tortured without your permission . . ."

"They can be questioned but not tortured!"

"How gentle you are Prince. I could almost think that you are courting death. Lord Forollkin, you are very silent."

To avoid staring at the Queen, Forollkin had fixed his attention on an alabaster lamp in the form of a half-open flower that hung above her head. Now he was forced to look at her.

"None of the *Zeloka*'s crew would be familiar with a Seldian mansion."

"Most of them have visited Seld several times before," replied the Queen, "and besides, a gate on the other side of the garden had been left open by workmen rebuilding a fountain. The archer only had to cross the garden and shoot from the terrace. Any Seldian would know that the garden would be empty in the heat of midday and a Galkian might guess."

Sensing that Pellameera already knew the answers, Forollkin said, "Your Majesty, I noticed that the Captain of our escort led us back to the palace by a different route to the one we'd taken to the harbour. Therefore the archer must have known our route in advance. Perhaps the Captain . . ."

"The Captain has been . . . questioned, but I do not suspect him. He was merely obeying my exact orders, delivered to him by Lord Djezaney."

"And your Majesty does suspect Lord Djezaney?"

The Queen seemed a little surprised at such a direct question, but she answered readily enough.

"Djezaney has often been a guest at the mansion of the Galkian Envoy. He has acquired more knowledge than befits a man, in Seld at least, and no doubt he has grown rich on bribes to use his influence."

"And has he any?" asked Forollkin bluntly.

Pellameera chose a green ribbon from a skein of coloured silks and began to plait it into her hair.

"I have humoured him in the past but he has more spirit than most of my courtiers and he begins to be dangerous. There are those in Seld who conspire against the rule of Queens and babble of having Kings again. Perhaps Djezaney has joined them. Lord Djan, who only desires my wealth to buy pretty clothes and trinkets, is a safer favourite. Perhaps I should rid myself of both of them . . . what do you advise?"

"I think, Lady," answered Kerish slowly, "that you should choose a favourite worthy to love you."

Pellameera laughed.

"Dear Prince, a Queen is never loved."

"That can't be true!" said Forollkin and then flinched under her cool green gaze.

"And a Queen never loves," murmured Pellameera, "though she may, most earnestly, desire a friend. So, Prince, you have two enemies in Galkis; your stepmother the Empress perhaps, or the Princess Zyrindella . . . I do not advise you to go home."

"I do not mean to until our quest is complete."

"Ah, this mysterious quest again!" Pellameera chose another ribbon to interweave with her copper hair. "Abandon it. You have proved your courage, you have escaped from Galkis. Why not settle here? Both of you would be welcome at my court."

"I think your Majesty already knows that I will not stay," answered Kerish, "but my brother must speak for himself . . ."

"It doesn't seem that he can," said Pellameera as Forollkin stared at her. "I will answer for him. Yes, he wants to stay but he would never be happy in Seld or with its wicked Queen."

"Your Majesty, I . . ."

"Say nothing, Forollkin," insisted Pellameera, "but try not to think too harshly of me. Now, Prince, you still wish to sail to Gannoth?"

"Yes, your Majesty." Kerish got up from the window seat. "We must speak to the King of Gannoth."

"That may not prove as easy as you think," said Pellameera, "but I see that nothing will daunt you. Ah, what it is to be young and eager for impossibilities. If I were not Queen of Seld I would bind up my hair and trudge after you, like your little cousin, on this great quest of yours. I am sending Lady Tirria to Gultim to represent me at the coronation of the King of Gannoth. You could sail with her . . ."

Kerish bowed, "We are grateful for your courtesy, but the *Zeloka* will be making the same voyage . . ."

"And you would rather journey in Galkian company? Very well. Both ships shall sail together in two days' time," said Pellameera. "I promised to show you my tomb. Tomorrow we will meet there and spend a few carefree hours before our parting."

Back at their apartments, the Galkians found Gidjabolgo gorging himself on their supper.

"Well, has the Queen hunted down your hidden archer?"

Forollkin sat down and poured himself some wine. "No he wasn't caught, but the Queen knows more than she's saying and there's little doubt that the man was acting under orders from Galkis."

Gidjabolgo glanced up at the Prince. "I'm grateful that I don't belong to such a close family. When do we sail for Gannoth?"

"The day after tomorrow," answered Forollkin. "Do you still want to journey with us? I suppose you could wait in Gannoth while we visit the Dead Kingdom."

"What, and deprive my masters of my valuable services? No, you won't shake me off so easily."

Unexpectedly, Kerish smiled. "I think you may be just what we need to keep us solid amongst the shadows of Roac."

"What am I but a servant of your needs?" asked Gidjabolgo and bit into his third honey cake.

The next morning the Queen's guests were escorted to the Royal Tombs. Gwerath had tried on several dresses before reverting to her Erandachi clothes but she had bound her hair with ribbon of Seldian silk. As they walked side by side along a tiled path, Forollkin asked the Princess what she thought of Mel-Kellin. Gwerath glanced along a glossy wall, delicately stippled in blue and gold, and up at the nearest of the twelve gaudy and fragile castles.

"When Kerish told me about cities, I thought that I would feel the oldness of them. I thought I would feel the weight of so many seasons, so many happenings in one place, but this," said Gwerath contemptuously, "this is just like Erandachu. It is pretty but they tear down their wooden houses when they tire of them, like the Sheyasa move camp. There is nothing here to feel."

"Perhaps the tombs will be more to your taste," suggested Gidjabolgo. "Their owners have no choices left."

Enclosed by a featureless white wall, the Royal Tombs of Seld were built in sombre black stone. Each of them was carved in the shape of a crowned head, a portrait of the Queen it entombed. To Kerish they looked like vast statues buried up to their necks in the earth with eyes that beseeched him to free them. Pellameera's tomb was only half-finished. The lower part of the head was still unpolished and the door was not yet concealed amongst the coils of stone hair. Inside, the walls were decorated with a series of portraits of the Queen from her childhood to her present age and the roughly hewn floor of the tomb chamber had been strewn with flowers and embroidered cushions. On the spot where she would one day lie, stripped of everything but a black winding sheet, Pellameera sat on a throne of ivory. Her courtiers clustered around her and Djan knelt at her feet. Lord Djezaney was missing.

The Queen welcomed her guests and invited them to admire the painted walls. Kerish responded sincerely, for the artist had snared Pellameera's distinctive beauty, but Forollkin shuddered to think of those bright images smiling through the darkness at shrouded bones. The painter and the sculptors of the tomb were brought forward to be praised and rewarded by the Queen and her courtiers.

"How fast the work progresses!" murmured Pellameera. "One might almost think it was a matter of urgency."

No-one answered her, and after an uneasy pause the Queen asked her guests to sit down on the cushions heaped to the right of her throne.

Wine and sweetmeats were brought for the men and the nobility of Seld began to laugh and chatter, unoppressed by the torchlit tomb. For the travellers' amusement Lord Djan and another nobleman competed in a Dwyhak. This proved to be something between a dance and a game. One player performed a series of ritual movements in an order of his own choosing while the other rhythmically tossed flowers at him, scoring points when they struck home. It was pretty but absurd and Kerish marvelled at the Queen's apparent delight in such a spectacle.

Next, the ladies of the court improvised short poems chosen by the Queen. Kerish could just manage to join in and produced a passable verse on the transience of beauty, but the other three were tongue-tied. Then Pellameera beckoned to a lady who had been sitting close to the throne with a small stringed instrument across her lap.

"The Court Poet has devised a song in honour of your deeds. Will you hear it, Prince?"

Kerish could hardly refuse, so the poet tuned her instrument and sang of the defeat of the evil Saroc and the destruction of dread Tir-Tonar by the Prince of Galkis and his gallant brother. The two Galkians listened in growing discomfort to a grossly distorted account of their deeds in the Red Waste.

"Are you pleased with your praises?" asked Pellameera

over the ripple of applause as the song ended.

"I would be pleased more by the truth," answered Kerish.

"What, sung in public? Surely not. Be grateful that the lies are in your favour; you should hear some of the songs they sing about me . . . Ah, I see the Wardress. Here is some truth for you, Prince. Bring him in!"

A woman, clad in black mail with a bunch of iron keys at her waist, was standing in the doorway. At the Queen's command she stepped aside and two soldiers entered half-carrying the slumped body of a man. At a nod from the Wardress they threw him down at Pellameera's feet. The man's wrists were manacled, his clothes torn and stained and his face swollen by bruises. It was only by his crooked hand that the travellers recognized Lord Djezaney.

"Here is his confession, your Majesty."

The Wardress handed Pellameera a parchment stamped with Djezaney's seal. The Queen read it calmly and there was complete silence in the burial chamber until she folded the parchment again.

"The prisoner confesses to treacherous thoughts against my Majesty and my government. Ah, what ingratitude in one I favoured so generously . . ."

There were hasty exclamations of distress and indignation from her white-faced courtiers. Satisfied, Pellameera continued, "And the prisoner further confesses to conspiring with . . . certain parties to arrange the murder of our cherished guest, the Prince of Galkis, in return for five thousand gold pieces to be used in stirring discontent amongst my subjects. Did he confess this freely?"

"Upon slight persuasion," said the Wardress with a grim smile.

Pellameera offered the parchment to the Prince, but he shook his head.

"I do not choose to know."

"As you will," said Pellameera, though she knew that Forollkin was longing to snatch the parchment from her. "How do you advise me to treat this traitor?"

"Banish him," suggested Kerish, looking away from the ruined face.

"I think not," murmured the Queen. "He is only a man and easily corrupted, so I forgive his offences against my crown, but there can be no mercy for his crime against you, or what could I say to the Emperor your brother? He must die today. Djezaney!"

The soldiers dragged him to his feet, but his eyes were closed by bruises and he could not look at her.

"Djezaney, how would you like to die?"

The Seldian tried to answer, but his mouth was full of blood.

"If you can't speak, I will choose and because of my affection for you, I will honour you, even in death." Pellameera untied the white sash from her slender waist and handed it to one of the soldiers. "Strangle him with this."

Kerish jumped to his feet as the soldiers seized Djezaney's dark curls and tilted back his head and Forollkin protested, "Not here, your Majesty!"

"What fitter place? But if the sight of a just death offends you . . . Take him outside!"

Djezaney was dragged from the tomb and the Queen ordered her musicians to play.

"Ah, how cruelly I am treated!" With an elaborate sigh, Pellameera drew her ice-green cloak about her shoulders. "Among all my Lords, can I believe that there is one who loves his Queen?"

Lord Djan, paler than the lace at his wrists, crouched to kiss the hem of the Queen's cloak.

"My love for your Majesty is greater than all Zindar!"

"Then Zindar is a little world and I am Queen of nothing. Dear Prince, will you dance with me again? This will be our last celebration together, for no doubt this afternoon you will wish to attend the burial of the Galkian Envoy. Ah, did I forget to mention his death?" asked Pellameera. "A sad accident . . ."

"You did," said Kerish curtly.

"Don't be angry over such a trifling fault," pleaded the Queen. "We may never meet again."

Finally the Prince agreed and Forollkin always remembered Pellameera as she looked then, dancing in the shadow of her death.

Chapter 4

The Book of the Emperors: *Warnings*
*All men, in greater and lesser degrees, possess the power of
illusion and use it often against those they love.*

THE great chain that barred the mouth of the Rellendon
was lifted, allowing the *Zeloka* and the royal ship of
Seld to sail out into the straits of Gannoth where the pale
turquoise of the Dirian Sea mingled with the turbulent
waters of the Great Ocean.

All morning Gwerath hung over the ship's rail watching
the sea-birds and the white-flecked waves. Battling against
queasiness, Forollkin was slightly irritated to notice that
Gwerath was not at all affected by the plunging ship.

"You seem to like the sea, cousin."

"Like?" Gwerath was contemptuous of so tame a word.
"The sea is too fierce to be liked. It is beautiful and wild and
dangerous like the hunting cats of the plains. It is all I hoped
it would be. I wish I could live by the sea."

"Wouldn't you miss your grasslands?"

"No." Gwerath's face closed up like a flower at dusk.
"No, I don't ever want to see plains or mountains again."

"And I don't want to see another royal court," said
Forollkin heartily, "but Zeldin and Imarko, it's good to be
on board a Galkian ship again!"

He glanced up at the purple and golden sails and the
Galkian sailors singing to the wind as they scrambled
through the rigging.

"You are glad to leave Seld then?" asked Gwerath.

"Of course," answered Forollkin, but she noticed the
second's hesitation before he spoke.

The funeral of the Galkian Envoy had been a sombre and

56

disquieting ceremony and afterwards there had been a grim feast in the Galkian Embassy. Forollkin had drunk rather too much and argued with Gwerath, who had insisted that Pellameera had been right to have the man killed. Kerish had been forced to talk very loudly to his neighbour to cover their angry and indiscreet whispers.

"I would guess that the court of Gannoth will be very different from Seld. It's only a small island," said Forollkin as Kerish came round the deck carrying a cloak for Gwerath. The wind was rising and the cold green waters of the Great Ocean seemed to chill the ship.

"A small island," agreed Kerish, "but I've heard it said that Gultim is the most ancient city in Zindar. I've always wanted to see it. After all, I'm part Gannothan and so are you, Forollkin."

"I'd forgotten that. The Emperor's mother was a Princess of Gannoth, Gwerath, but she died before either of us was born."

"She pricked her finger on a thorn in the Emperor's garden," said Kerish. "She died within an hour and the thorn tree blossomed for the first time in memory. Forollkin, Engis wanted to see you about something."

When his brother had gone to the poop deck, Kerish persuaded Gwerath to wear the fleece cloak.

"I can see you're going to be like me and get in everyone's way on deck till you've found out how things work. When you get bored, come to my cabin and I can show you more books and scrolls. We could start writing lessons again and I could teach you the zildar . . ."

"I don't think . . . I don't think I want to."

She would have moved away from him but Kerish gripped her wrists.

"You mustn't stop wanting things! Gwerath, can't we be friends again? What happened between Forollkin and me is something for the two of us alone, though I promise you couldn't blame me more than I do myself."

"I know I don't understand how Forollkin feels about you," said Gwerath stiffly. "You don't have to tell me that."

"And about the Goddess, please believe that we were

57

only trying to protect you and I do know how you must feel . . ."

"But I don't want you to know how I feel!" shouted Gwerath. "Can't I have anything to myself?"

"I'm sorry," said Kerish blankly. "I'm sorry."

The next morning, after they had breakfasted with the Captain, and were standing on the poop deck watching a shoal of fish following the ship, Gwerath turned to Kerish.

"Will you call me Princess of the Sheyasa in Gannoth?" Kerish nodded. "Then perhaps I should learn to be a Princess. Would you still teach me Galkian and how to write, and play the zildar, or are you angry with me now?"

"I'm not angry," said Kerish in a puzzled voice. "When do you want to start?"

"Now, please, now."

For the next two days Gwerath sat in the Prince's cabin learning the Galkian alphabet and trying to read simple passages of Zindaric he wrote down for her. Sometimes she worked feverishly, sometimes she seemed to forget Kerish's existence and sank into deep silences. During the music lessons, Gidjabolgo joined them and watched with amusement as Kerish struggled to teach Gwerath simple chords. She was not naturally musical and her fingers seemed to stumble over the easiest combinations. To reward her efforts Kerish would play for her, and for Gidjabolgo, and sing till his throat ached. Forollkin never once joined them. He talked to Engis, strode round the deck, or kept to his cabin.

It was there that Kerish found him on the second evening when he wanted to search through part of their luggage for a spare string to his zildar. Forollkin had been sitting on his bunk, re-reading the letter from his mother. As Kerish came in he crumpled it in his hands.

"I'm not surprised you've broken a string. You'll snap a finger next with all that music."

"You don't mind my playing, do you?"

"Mind? You block my ears with your wailing tunes and then ask if I mind."

Kerish found a string and sat down beside his brother, with the zildar across his lap.

"I'm only trying to entertain Gwerath."

"Well, there's an easy audience. She doesn't notice what you play to her."

"Gwerath has a natural appreciation of what is good . . ."

"And I suppose I haven't."

"I didn't mean that."

Kerish bent over his zildar and tried to change the subject before his exasperation showed.

"I have been wondering how much we should tell the King of Gannoth. He might try to stop us entering the Dead Kingdom and risking our lives."

"Well no doubt your golden tongue will beguile him."

Kerish deftly knotted the new string. "I shall try to persuade him."

"Persuade? I often wonder if that's all, now I know what you can do. Still if you can persuade him to look after Gwerath for us . . ."

"That would make her very unhappy."

Forollkin stretched out on the bed, frowning up at the swinging lamp. "Unhappy and safe. Do you want her killed?"

"I want her to have something to live for. You don't understand how important our quest has become to Gwerath."

"I have better things to do than worry about understanding Gwerath."

"No you don't," said Kerish angrily. "If just for once you would use what little imagination you have . . ."

"Kerish, I will not be shouted at by you . . ."

"I'm sorry." The Prince slammed a hand against the cabin wall. "I swore I'd be patient with you but, Forollkin, for Zeldin's sake, what's the matter with you?"

Forollkin sat up and looked into his brother's anxious eyes.

"Kerish, I'm sorry too. I should have talked to you about it, but I suppose I still like to think of you as my little brother who mustn't be troubled with foolish passions that

59

he wouldn't understand. Now, I'm the fool for refusing to let you grow away from what you were, and for letting my eyes betray me to Pellameera."

Kerish listened while Forollkin talked about the beauty and the cruelty of the Queen of Seld.

"Well, I've told you now and I mean to stop thinking about her. She wasn't worth remembering."

"I think you misjudge her," said Kerish. "Pellameera is clever and brave. It's the crown of Seld that has made her cruel. Without it she might have been worthy of your love."

"You only say that to make me feel less stupid. I hope you never get tangled in such feelings. If you do, I'll always be here to listen but I suppose you'd be too proud to talk about it."

"Yes." Kerish finished replacing the string.

"Well," said Forollkin, "you're right. I ought to be trying to cheer our little cousin. I haven't seen her laugh since we left the Sheyasa."

They went back together to Kerish's cabin and Forollkin taught Gwerath one of the simpler Galkian board games; played six rounds with her and talked for minutes on end about his service on the Tryfanian border. Gwerath listened intently; lost every game and smiled at her defeats.

The next morning, the *Zeloka* and the Seldian ship entered the harbour of Gultim, the only city of Gannoth. The harbour was already crowded with the ships of envoys from Dard and Losh, Forgin, Further Eran, Kolgor and Chiraz. Kerish and Forollkin hurried on deck to catch their first glimpse of mountainous Gannoth and of Gultim itself.

The city was massively built in blue-grey stone to withstand the winter gales and lay on a steep slope, dominated by the gaunt palace of the Lords of Gannoth. There were no streets, only endless flights of steps and even the most exalted traveller was forced to go on foot.

As the *Zeloka* dropped anchor, a guard of honour was assembling on the quay.

"Ah, the Prince has sent his Great Steward to meet us," said Engis.

"The Prince?"

"Prince Hemcoth, my Lord."

"Is the King in seclusion before his coronation?" asked Kerish.

"Seclusion? Indeed he is. Forgive me, I thought your Highness knew the customs of Gannoth. The King is dead."

"Dead!" exclaimed Forollkin. "Have we come to a burial then?"

"No, my Lord. The Gannothans believe that the Crown Prince only becomes king when he dies and rules through his son, the new Crown Prince. They say it is a very ancient custom."

Engis started to explain further and then stopped in the middle of a sentence as Gwerath came on deck.

The Princess of the Sheyasa wore a Seldian dress of pale turquoise. She had spent a long time binding up her hair and only a few stubborn wisps still straggled down her slim neck. Engis bowed. Forollkin smiled approvingly and Kerish gave her his hand to lead her ashore.

They were preceded by a herald who announced to the welcoming party the unavoidable absence of the Galkian Envoy and the arrival of Prince Kerish-lo-Taan with his brother, the Lord Forollkin, and his cousin, the Princess Gwerath. The Great Steward truthfully proclaimed himself overwhelmed by the unexpected honour and sent a messenger racing up to the Palace with orders to rearrange the guest chambers. He bowed very low to the Prince and alarmed Gwerath by kissing the hem of her robe. She looked plaintively at Kerish who answered the formal welcome for her. There was a brief wait while the Ambassadress of Seld and her party were greeted. Then the Great Steward led them all up a steep flight of steps strewn with aromatic herbs.

Pale, brooding faces appeared at dark windows as the Gannothans stared at the strangers with mute curiosity. The Great Steward paused frequently during their slow climb through the sombre city to point out worn inscriptions and paintings, half-stripped away by the salty air. Kerish guessed that the old man was delaying their arrival so that their rooms could be made ready.

Finally the Great Steward brought the travellers to a grim mansion built at the foot of the Palace wall, announcing that he would return in an hour to escort them to the royal banquet that began the coronation ceremonies. When their luggage had been brought up from the ship, Kerish and Forollkin changed into Galkian finery in a gloomy chamber, hung with musty tapestries and furnished in the fashion of centuries before.

Since Gidjabolgo was included in the invitation he dressed up in gaudy silks acquired in Seld and admired the effect in a hand-mirror while Kerish delved in one of the carrying-chests and brought out an ivory casket.

"Come back!" ordered Forollkin. "Your fillet's crooked. Stand still while I straighten it."

"I thought I'd take Gwerath a jewel to wear at the feast," said Kerish meekly.

"And I was beginning to think you weren't playing to win," murmured Gidjabolgo.

Forollkin ignored him. "That's a good idea. Our poor cousin brought so little with her from Erandachu."

At first Gwerath refused to accept the necklace of moonflowers. "No, I couldn't wear something so beautiful!"

"It was made for my mother, for Taana, and you are her brother's daughter. Wear it and keep it."

Gwerath touched the cool gems for a moment and then let Kerish fasten them around her throat.

"Thank you, cousin. I will wear it and think of her."

Moments later the Great Steward was announced and he asked permission to lead them to the feast. Kerish took Gwerath's hand again and Forollkin and Gidjabolgo followed behind with Engis and an escort of Galkian sailors.

The Palace was built of the same sombre stone as the city below but the Galkians marvelled at the skill of the builders, who had placed its squat towers and massive keep on a narrow promontory of jagged rock. The walls had once been richly decorated with sculptures but the stormy centuries had half-destroyed the reliefs and statues. Their almost shapeless figures, symbols of a long, losing battle with the elements, gave the Palace an air of melancholy antiquity.

The travellers were led through a dark tunnel into a courtyard where the sculptures were partly sheltered from wind and rain. Twelve great stone ships survived, with only patches of lichen to obscure the elaborate detail of hull and mast and sails. The walls of the courtyard were engraved with the sun, the moon and stars, while the floor had been carved with wave-like patterns, now almost worn away by constant footsteps.

The Great Steward hurried them on and up a broad flight of stairs into the hall of the Prince's Palace, where they stepped from darkness into the glow of a hundred torches.

As his titles were announced, Kerish-lo-Taan walked the length of the hall towards the dais to be greeted by Prince Hemcoth and his sister, the Princess Mekotta. He noticed at once Hemcoth's frail physique and ashen hair and the unnatural pallor of his eyes. The Princess shared her brother's colouring but her features were more definite, as if the bones were stronger.

Kerish was seated in the place of honour and Gwerath came forward, the torches drawing splinters of light from the frosted gems at her throat. In the privacy of her cabin she had been practising a curtsey, and she sank down in a graceful whisper of silk. As Hemcoth raised her up, Gwerath saw that he was no older than Kerish, and his gentle face and hesitant speech almost conquered her nervousness. She answered him calmly, in spite of the watching crowd of Gannothans, and took her place beside Mekotta.

Finally, Forollkin, Gidjabolgo, and Engis were presented and all placed at the high table. Their neighbours were Lords and Ladies of Gannoth, shivering in the thin, pleated robes they wore beneath embroidered tabards, which had been handed down from generation to generation. At the lower tables sat the other envoys. The severe Ambassadress of Seld was placed beside the silent, dark-skinned envoy of Kolgor and his attendants. In another group were a feather-cloaked Count of Dard and a Merchant Prince of Forgin, while two grim warriors of Chiraz were uneasily

63

seated next to the smiling, heavily perfumed Ambassador of Losh.

All of them were watching the Galkians with undisguised curiosity but the Merchant also stared at Gidjabolgo. Kerish noticed that the Forgite was scowling worse than usual but he had no opportunity to ask what was wrong.

A single bronze bell rang out and the feast began. The faded hangings to one side of the hall parted and out came a procession of pages carrying platters of fish and dishes piled with the eggs of sea-birds, dyed with coloured spices. As the first page reached the high table he was suddenly transformed: green scales covered his face, and fins, not hands, held out the silver platter.

"I hope, Princess," said Hemcoth, "that these slight illusions will not trouble you."

With shaking hands, Gwerath accepted a cup from the paws of a whiskered creature, draped in seaweed. It bowed and turned back into a page.

"No," said Gwerath boldly, "it is a pretty game."

"A game? Yes, I suppose your Highness is right to call it a game."

Hemcoth's lips were as pale as his eyes and hair; only his restless hands seemed imbued with energy.

"These transformations were devised some centuries ago for the amusement of one of my ancestors and now it is my duty to continue them."

Gwerath refused a helping of fish from a creature with shells for eyes and asked, "Is it your power that makes them change?"

"My slight power, yes. I haven't the strength to deceive your eyes for long. My sister could do better but she does not care for the grotesque."

He smiled affectionately at Mekotta who, in between talking to Forollkin about the crossing from Seld, watched her brother anxiously.

"No, I do not care for your ugly marvels, nor I'm sure do our guests. The Galkians are famous for their love of beauty."

"I am glad we still have such a reputation," answered Kerish, "but remember, your Highness, that Forollkin and

I have Gannothan blood."

"The Princess Zillela is well remembered in Gannoth," said Hemcoth. "Her powers were very strong. Yet like all our line she was only mistress of illusion. She could alter nothing."

"Men's minds can be influenced by illusion," answered Kerish, "and surely that is more important than any power over physical things."

"We long for power over the sea," murmured Hemcoth, staring down at the silvery fish curled on his plate, "but we are helpless on our barren rock and must bow before the wind."

"On the eve of a coronation the wind always drops away," said Mekotta. "You cannot imagine how strange it is for us not to hear the wind howling at our gates."

The Prince and Princess fell silent as if someone had spoken their dead father's name.

Kerish shelled a purple egg; Gwerath sipped thin wine from the mountainous vineyards of Gultim; Forollkin stared down the smoky hall and Gidjabolgo attacked his plate of fish with relish.

"Forgive me," said Hemcoth after a few minutes, "this is a cruel season for us. I know you will understand, having celebrated the death of your honoured father so recently."

Hemcoth was too polite to enquire the reason for Kerish's journey but he did ask him to describe his travels.

"And Galkis too. I am bound to my island kingdom and can never visit the Golden City but I have often read about it. I have a copy of the Book of the Emperors, presented by your grandfather to mine."

For a short while Kerish talked about Galkis but even as he described the great cities, temples and palaces, they seemed as distant and insubstantial as inventions of his own fancy.

The best wine was brought round with dishes of sweet berries and the grave nobility of Gannoth became a little more animated. Acrobats performed in the middle of the hall, their leaping bodies transformed into grotesque and fanciful shapes by the watching Masters of Illusion. The guests looked on with pleasure but Hemcoth seemed bored

65

with the acrobats and irritated by the monotonous drumbeats that accompanied their performance.

He turned to Gwerath and asked her to describe Erandachu. At first she spoke very hesitantly but Hemcoth's eager questions and the absurdity of the legends he had heard about the Children of the Wind persuaded her to describe the Sheyasa and their customs. Kerish noticed that she mentioned the Hunter of Souls but said nothing about the Mountain Goddess.

"Please forgive my ignorance, Princess," begged Hemcoth, "and I will write down all you say in my book."

"My brother loves listening to travellers," said Mekotta, "and he writes down all their descriptions of Zindar, however fanciful they may be."

"Well some are no more than legends, it's true, but it is fascinating to discover how other men imagine distant places."

"To us, Gannoth is a place of legend," said Kerish. "In Galkis it is said that Gultim is the most ancient city in Zindar."

"Indeed it is, and it is only here that the riddle of men's coming into Zindar can be answered." Hemcoth waved excited hands at the dull tapestries. "Once those hangings were woven with the images of eleven men and one woman, each with a ship in their hands. There are twelve ships in the courtyard and I am sure they represent the ships that brought the first men into Zindar, from across the Great Ocean."

"But where did they come from?" demanded Forollkin.

"Ah, once the courtyard could have told us. The paving stones are patterned like the sea and there are still faint lines that mark the land. It's a map, a chart, but so much is worn away."

"So the knowledge they meant to leave us is lost."

"Not quite, your Highness," said Hemcoth, "they left something else to be guarded by my ancestors. After the coronation, I will take you to the Cave of Pictures."

"Hemcoth, you will be too tired!"

The Prince brushed aside his sister's objection.

"Please come, and then you can tell me whether you

think my guesses about the past of Zindar are right or wrong."

"We should be honoured," said Kerish, "and we have heard some legends about the coming of men that might interest you."

"Yes, if we join our knowledge . . ."

The bronze bell rang again and a soft whisper from Mekotta reminded Hemcoth of his duties. He rose and offered his hand to Gwerath and Mekotta walked beside Kerish. Forollkin and Gidjabolgo followed among the foreign guests, who were led up a crumbling flight of steps to the Palace ramparts.

As they took their places on stone benches, the Envoy of Forgin approached them.

"My Lord of Galkis, may a humble merchant greet you?"

Forollkin bowed stiffly. The merchant tugged absently at the longest of his pearl necklaces.

"I merely wished to inquire how your Lordship enjoyed the humour of my Fool. I must congratulate your Lordship on dressing him so richly, a most amusing idea, though of course the cost . . ."

"The humble merchant refers to a period when I was in his service," said Gidjabolgo.

"Be quiet, Fool, when I am talking to your Master," snapped the Envoy. "He was always insufferably insolent, my Lord. I was not sorry to have him leave my household on some mad errand, but as a grotesque he is a fine specimen. I have never seen better, even in the market of Losh, yet I never had a servant who invited beatings more often. I trust your Lordship beats him harder than my tender hand could ever do . . ."

Forollkin was too startled by the merchant's rapid speech to reply but Kerish had overheard and he turned round angrily.

"We do not beat our friends, Merchant."

The Envoy of Forgin knelt and began to express his joy at the Prince's condescension in addressing him.

"I address you," said Kerish, "only to have you understand that Master Gidjabolgo is our faithful and

67

valiant companion."

"Companion?" The merchant was obviously bewildered but at the look on the Prince's face he stammered out a lengthy apology and withdrew.

"Faithful and valiant?" repeated Gidjabolgo. "My Master lies as prettily as a courtesan of Losh."

"The Godborn never lie," said Kerish, with his most winning smile, "so you had better make my words true."

When the Gannothans and their guests were settled on the rows of stone benches the single bronze bell sounded again. The night was unnaturally still: there was no breath of wind and at the foot of the hill the sea lay tamely, glossed by moonlight.

From among the Gannothans, six Masters of Illusion stepped forward, each one cloaked and hooded in white. Hemcoth bound their eyes with strips of white silk and stopped their ears with balls of wax. Then he lifted his arms and cried out a few words in an ancient form of Zindaric.

The bronze bell in the highest tower of the Palace began to toll; a second bell answered it from one of the mansions below the walls; and then a third and a fourth. Soon, every bell in the city was ringing and the people of Gultim came out on to their stepped streets or crowded at open windows.

As the bells rang louder and louder a shadow seemed to creep across the moon. Hemcoth whispered to Gwerath that she needn't be afraid. She almost answered him sharply but then the moon was engulfed and the shadow spread across the stars. It became entirely dark, and one by one the bells ceased.

The Gannothans looked up expectantly at the sky but Gwerath could see nothing. Then the Masters of Illusion raised their arms, linked hands and spread the ancient pageant of the Kings of Gannoth across the night skies.

At first there was only a white centre to the darkness, and then the whiteness coalesced into the shape of a bird, a huge creature whose wings spanned the heavens. The bird seemed to swoop over the Palace and vanished with a haunting cry.

Next came the vast figure of a man. His clothes were

stained and ragged but he carried a blue staff and wore a crystal crown. For a moment the man towered above Gultim and then he turned to his right and faded into the darkness.

Already a second figure was approaching. His clothes were richer, but he carried the same staff and wore the same crown. For an instant every grim detail of his face was visible. Then he, too, vanished and a third crowned figure appeared.

Gwerath soon lost count of the pale-haired kings who overawed the night. Then beside her she heard Kerish gasp. He was staring at the sky as if he were seeing something far more terrible but after a moment he seemed to feel her gaze. He relaxed his clenched hands and smiled at her as the great pageant continued.

At last, one figure appeared who wore no crown and carried no staff. His face seemed wracked with pain and he stretched out his hands in one vast, silent gesture of despair before fading into darkness. Then the great bell rang again and the bells of the city answered.

Moonlight filtered through the darkness, destroying the illusion and glinting on the tears streaming down Mekotta's cheeks. The ceremony over, the Prince took his sister's hand and quietly bade their guests goodnight.

As the Great Steward led the travellers back to their apartments Gwerath whispered to Kerish: "Are you ill? You looked as if something was hurting you."

"No, not ill, I saw . . . I felt the High Priest of Zeldin leaving."

"Leaving?"

"Dying," murmured Kerish, "but Gwerath, I saw his face and he wasn't afraid."

"Was he someone close to you?" asked Gwerath.

"Close? Yes," said Kerish, "then and now."

At dawn the Prince and his companions were summoned again to the Great Hall of the Palace. Engis went with them, adding whispered comments to the instructions of the Great Steward as they took their place in front of the faded tapestries.

"Your Highness will see that they are marvellously skilful in preserving their dead. Many's the time I've walked along the cliffs among their tombs and thought . . ." What Engis thought was cut off by the entry of a strange procession.

First came a young man carrying a hooded bird at his wrist.

"The King's hunting gethon," murmured Engis but Kerish was not looking at the white bird, for the Prince and Princess of Gannoth came next and between them, in a chair carried by two sea-captains, was their father. The body of the King was swathed in rich brocades. The arms were stretched out in front of him and the stiff hands were held open, as if, even in death, there was something he longed to grasp.

The King's skin was so tightly stretched over the bones that there seemed to be no flesh between and the shrunken eye sockets were filled with pieces of crystal. Gwerath couldn't bear the glitter of that unnatural gaze for more than a moment and she was not the only visitor to turn away, or clutch a scented handkerchief.

Behind the King's chair came two more grey-cloaked captains, one carrying the crystal crown, the other, the blue staff. Last of all came a child of six or seven years, dressed in white and looking very shy and solemn.

The King's chair was set down and Hemcoth and Mekotta knelt before it. A page brought forward a bowl of sea-water and, after a little prompting, the child dipped his hands in the bowl and anointed the Prince and his sister.

Then, hesitantly, the child approached the chair and its grimly smiling occupant. Hemcoth gently lifted him up so that he could anoint the dead King's forehead.

A long chant was sung in ancient Zindaric and the captains offered the crown and the staff to the child. He put the staff in the King's hands and Hemcoth closed the dead fingers around it. The crown was almost too heavy for the child to lift but with Hemcoth's help he placed it on the King's head and the Gannothans crowded round to kiss the stiff brocade of the royal robe. The child was taken away and the first part of the ceremony was over.

Hemcoth was very pale and his hands clutched nervously

at his pleated robes. It was Mekotta who gave the order to proceed. The chair was lifted again and a slow procession left the hall. Kerish and his companions walked behind the Great Steward and the other guests followed, their faces marked with boredom or distaste.

They left the Palace and the city and walked in silence along the western cliffs till they reached a headland overlooking the Great Ocean. Below, the cliffs were white with sea-birds and the air should have been full of their raucous screaming. Instead, they were still and quiet. So were the Gannothans of the nearby villages who had crowded on to the green slopes above the headland and stood waiting with impassive faces.

Near to the edge of the cliff was a line of white tombs shaped like thrones. Through slits in the stone the dead Kings still looked out into the world and before every tomb was an altar piled with decaying offerings. Kerish found the still crowd, the silent birds, and the muted roar of the sea, horribly oppressive.

The King's chair was set down in front of a tomb that seemed only half complete. Hemcoth and Mekotta placed offerings on every altar and when they reached their father's tomb stooped to kiss his withered cheeks. The first Captain took back the crystal crown and the second wrenched the blue staff from the fierce grip of the dead hands.

In return, the new King was given a crudely painted staff and a crown of glass. The hunting gethon was fastened to the King's wrist and the chair was lifted up and placed inside the tomb. Masons came forward and began to fit the last blocks of white stone. Disturbed by the noise, the bird ruffled its pale feathers and dug its talons into the fleshless hand.

When only one gap remained in the white wall, Hemcoth reached into the tomb, released the bird and pulled off its hood. The gethon fluttered out into the daylight, spread its wings and soared upwards. The Gannothans watched intently and murmured with pleasure when the bird flew, not towards Gultim, but westwards across the Great Ocean. The last block was lifted into position, so that only a slit remained open, and the tomb was sealed.

With an unearthly shriek, a wind sprang up and all along the cliffs the sea-birds began to scream and chatter. Heavy fleece cloaks were brought forward and gratefully accepted by the visitors, for the ceremonies were not yet over.

Prince Hemcoth knelt in front of his father's tomb, facing the sea. The Gannothans began a chant. At first it was almost lost beneath the keening wind but gradually the slow insistent humming became more audible, as if it was absorbing all other sounds. The same tune, the same senseless words, were repeated over and over again as Mekotta poured wine on the altar of her father, splashing her white robes with crimson.

Kerish watched as the remaining colour faded from Hemcoth's skin and his breathing became unnaturally fast.

"Now the King will possess his son," whispered Engis, "and give oracles through him."

Hemcoth's frail body became rigid, the muscles of his face twitched uncontrollably, and his lips twisted into an incongruous grin. His eyes bulged and sweat poured down his brow as he gasped out a name.

"Kerish-lo-Taan."

Kerish hesitated and the Prince of Gannoth screamed. Mekotta ran to him.

"Please accept the oracle! He isn't strong enough to bear the pressure of the dead!"

Kerish knelt between the cliff edge and the tomb and gripped Hemcoth's hands.

"Roac, Roac." The words seemed to be pushed through an unseen barrier. "Take light to enfold the dark. Koandor, Koandor, through the dead waters, death to the ships of Zindar. Your ship must have its roots in a different earth, blue against black, Roac, Roac. Prince." Hemcoth's voice was suddenly clear and loud. "Turn back, the dark will take more than you can give."

Kerish shooks his head. "I can't. What . . . where is Koandor?"

Hemcoth's head lolled forward and his eyes closed. Then his body jerked, his face contorted and he whispered another name.

The gentle pressure of Mekotta's hand on his shoulder

72

roused Kerish. He walked away from the edge of the cliff as a Gannothan shepherd hurried forward to kneel before his Prince. "What did he say to you?" whispered Forollkin. "You look awful."

"Roac," murmured Kerish. "Later, I'll tell you later, just let me think."

The Galkians watched as six more Gannothans were called forward to receive oracles and Hemcoth grew visibly more and more exhausted.

At last the violent shuddering of his body stopped and the Prince slumped into a merciful faint. Mekotta tenderly wrapped a fleece cloak around her brother and he was carried back to the Palace on a litter. His guests followed, talking in groups of the strange and barbarous customs of Gannoth. Only the Prince of Galkis and his companions were silent.

Back at their lodgings the travellers had little appetite for the meal they were served. Kerish pushed aside a plate of pickled fish and crossed to one of the thin windows that let so little light into the gloomy dining chamber. With his back to the others, Kerish told them about the oracle.

None of them could make much sense of it and they were still arguing about what blue against black might mean when the Prince of Gannoth, unannounced and unattended, walked into the room. The shadows of pain and exhaustion still disfigured his face but he smiled serenely at his startled guests.

"No, truly, I am quite recovered. I have forgotten this morning, the only blessing that the burden of the oracle brings, but I have not forgotten my promise to show you the Cave of Pictures. It's an hour's walk from here. I hope it won't be too tiring for you, Princess."

"Tiring?" Gwerath was incredulous, but a nudge from Kerish made her say, "No, I'm sure not."

"Good, and my Lord Forollkin and Master Gidjabolgo, you are welcome too."

The Prince sent for warm cloaks and they took the quickest path out of the city and along the cliff tops. It appeared to be Hemcoth's custom to wander about his small realm without ceremony and he stopped to speak to every Gannothan they met.

"I have left my sister being polite to our other guests," confessed the Prince. "She's far better at it than I am. I never know what to say to those scowlers from Chiraz, let alone the Envoy of Losh."

He led the travellers along a lower path than they had taken that morning and greatly amused the Galkians by trying to help Gwerath over the slightest obstacle and continuously asking if she needed to rest. Occasionally, Gwerath agreed but only for the sake of the frail Prince.

As they rounded the headland, wind and sea made conversation more difficult and they walked in silence, preoccupied with holding on to their cloaks. Kerish looked up once, the wind stinging tears from his eyes, and saw the white tombs high above them.

Hemcoth took a path that led sharply down to the grey shore beneath the cliff of tombs. The tide was out, leaving the pebbled beach fully exposed. They walked across broken shells, slippery rocks and dank patches of clinging seaweed.

Suddenly Hemcoth stooped with an excited cry. "Look!" He picked up a smooth piece of wood, as blue as the royal staff. "Have you ever seen such a colour? It's like no wood that grows in Zindar. It drifts here from across the Great Ocean, from an unknown land."

Kerish stared at it fixedly, suddenly understanding part of the oracle but Forollkin was saying, "Do you think your people came from this unknown land?"

"I think all the races of Zindar did," answered Hemcoth, "I long with all my heart to fit out a great fleet and sail across the Ocean to find that land, but I cannot leave Gannoth."

"Oh surely if you want it so much it must be right," exclaimed Gwerath.

Hemcoth tucked the blue wood into his belt and shook his pale head.

"I have often run to meet my desire and stumbled over my duty. I cannot leave my people and my heritage."

He turned towards the cliffs and led the travellers through a low entrance into a cave. At first the floor was covered with rock pools and they had to pick their way carefully among jagged stones and slippery, evil-smelling seaweed. At the foot of a pebbled slope Hemcoth reached the limit of the light from the entrance.

He clapped his hands and they waited, shivering in the dank cold of the cave. After a minute they heard a rattle of pebbles and smelled smoke. An old man, pale as if he had never seen light, and clothed in matted furs, hobbled towards them, carrying two torches.

"This is Bekon, the Guardian of the Cave."

The old man gave his Prince a toothless smile but he would not speak. When he had handed over the torches he scuttled away like a sea-creature retreating into its shell.

Hemcoth led them up the slope into a second and much larger cave. Water dripped from its green roof but the walls were covered with carvings in low relief. They had once been painted, but only a few flakes of colour still clung to the stone. The carved scenes were crowded together and arranged in no obvious sequence but Hemcoth led the travellers straight to the furthest wall.

"This is a great battle, but not fought in Zindar."

He held his torch high so that the others could see the mass of figures fighting with axes and two-edged blades.

"Can you see the settlement burning?"

He pointed to the blurred outline of a fortress that seemed to be built from the trunks of huge trees.

"Now look at this figure, he seems to be a chieftain and his head-dress is very like our crystal crown. There are several scenes missing on this wall, but then he appears again, with other chieftains."

Forollkin had the other torch and he held it close to the wall but the rock was so blotched with damp he could only see the outline of the crown, a hand clasping a rod and the profile of a woman.

"Here he is a third time," said Hemcoth, "watching a ship being built. It looks like the Ocean vessels of the traders of Further Eran, and here are more ships."

The torches lit Hemcoth's eager face and a group of ships so clearly carved that even the devices on their sails were visible.

"That one could almost be the Winged Circle of Galkis,"

murmured Kerish, tracing the symbol with his fingertips.

Hemcoth had already darted to the next wall.

"Now here are the ships sailing."

"Why, there are hundreds of them."

"Yes, Princess, a great fleet, filled with men and women, children and even animals."

"Oh yes." Forollkin waved away the smoke from his torch and leaned forward. "That looks like a cat, there by the stern post, Kerish."

"The walls are too damaged here to see much," Hemcoth was saying, "but I think this was a storm scene. That forked line could be lightning."

He knelt among the damp pebbles. "Down here there are drowned bodies, floating on the waves."

The flickering torchlight picked out a woman's hair tangled with seaweed and one forlorn hand clutching at a broken mast.

Hemcoth got up and crossed to another wall and the others followed. "This is the fleet again, close to the land. I have studied all the maps I can find and I believe this is the south-west coast of Seld, where there are no safe harbours."

"Oh, how horrible," murmured Gwerath. Forollkin's torch had lit a carving of an emaciated woman and a dead child.

"I fear there must have been famine among the ships," said Hemcoth, "before they reached the end of their long voyage."

Kerish had moved on to the next scene.

"Isn't this Gannoth?"

"Yes. There is the bay of Gultim and they are hauling stones up the hillside to build the Palace of the first King. This last wall," sighed Hemcoth, "is the hardest to understand. I think a quarrel is shown here. Can you see the crowned figure striking another man? I believe that many ships sailed away from Gannoth, north to Seld and south to Losh and Proy, and men sped eastwards."

"Across the empty lands," murmured Forollkin.

"Empty? No," said Hemcoth. "I don't think so. High on this wall is the best of all the carvings. Hold up your torch, Forollkin. Can you see a river coiling round? That is the

Rellendon and those, I am told, are . . ."

"Watch trees," finished Kerish. "They're building a city among them, aren't they?"

For the first time Gidjabolgo broke his silence.

"What are those figures?"

"Ah, that is the great riddle," answered Hemcoth.

"They have wings as well as arms!" exclaimed Forollkin.

"And three eyes," whispered Kerish.

"Yet they are beautiful," said Hemcoth, "and better carved than all the rest. Look, one of the creatures is trailing a broken wing. This is the last scene of all. Can you make out two creatures on either side of a tunnel of trees? One is spreading its wings and raising its hands, as if it was forbidding anyone to enter."

"While the other beckons," said Kerish.

"Summoning the chosen through the golden archway," whispered Gidjabolgo, and they stared at each other.

"Perhaps. I don't know," said Hemcoth.

Suddenly the old guardian hobbled out of a crack in one of the walls and tugged at his Prince's sleeve.

"Ah, of course, the tide must be coming in."

As Hemcoth spoke, the others noticed that the muffled roar of the sea sounded closer.

"The lower cave floods. We will leave by the stair."

They followed the old man through the crack and up a stair hewn in the rock. After a hundred steps they came to the small, dark chamber where the guardian lived but he followed them up the rest of the stairway. Hemcoth thanked the old man as they emerged through a low archway on to a path on the other side of the bay. Blinking in the evening sunlight, the guardian took the torches and went back into the darkness.

"He was the Captain of the Gannothan fleet," said Hemcoth, "long before I was born. One night he misjudged his distance from the rocks that lie beyond these cliffs. His vessel foundered and only he was washed ashore. He has never left the cave since then."

They walked back to Gultim by a different route, passing through a village where women sat in front of their stone huts, weaving the fine hair of the hardy cazmor into

77

cloaks for the wealthy of Seld and Losh. A herdsman with his flock of bleating cazmor stopped to speak to his Prince about the price of winter fodder and children, with caps full of eggs gathered from the dangerous cliffs, clustered round the strangers.

"No doubt you find our lack of ceremony strange, after Galkis," said Hemcoth, "but we are a small country and poor. Nevertheless, I have some things in my library that might interest your Highness . . ."

"I should be very glad to see your library," answered Kerish warmly, "and I hope you may be able to solve a riddle for us."

"A riddle?" Hemcoth's face brightened. "I will certainly try."

Kerish and his companions sat impatiently through the feast for the departing envoys and ambassadors and as soon as it was over they were taken to Prince Hemcoth's library in the highest tower of the Palace.

The wind howled round the massive walls and Mekotta, shivering in her thin robes, had just sat down beside the driftwood fire. Hemcoth was leaning over the central table, perilously close to a candle, trying to impose some order on a pile of books and scrolls. The room lacked the shabby grandeur of the rest of the palace and was as plain as any scholar's study.

Mekotta invited Gwerath to sit beside her. In spite of some misgivings about a Princess who travelled with no female companions, she was determined to be kind. So Gwerath was forced to talk about Erandachi clothes and her impressions of the court of Seld while trying to listen to what the others were saying.

Hemcoth began by showing them drawings he had made over the years of the carvings in the Cave of Pictures. Then he got out a map of the Dirian Sea and the adjoining coastlands to trace a possible route for the first ships. Kerish's finger flew to a small, thin island off the mountainous coast of Chiraz.

"Can you read the inscriptions?" asked Hemcoth. "That's Silnarnin."

"Then that," said Kerish, "is where we must go: to

Silnarnin and the Citadel of Tir-Melidon."

"I have never heard that Silnarnin was inhabited. In fact," continued Hemcoth, "I believe the cliffs make it impossible to land there. Look, there is no harbour marked on the map."

"We must try," murmured Kerish.

He was already looking at another part of the map: at Roac, but the Dead Kingdom was marked in solid black.

"Hemcoth, what are the Dead Waters?"

Mekotta faltered in the middle of a sentence and Hemcoth looked suddenly grim.

"The stuff of my nightmares," he answered. "Roac is a closed kingdom. Long ago a King of Roac became a great sorcerer and risked some forbidden danger that killed all his people, killed the land itself and the very sea that laps against Roac. Only he was left and some think he still survives, trapped in his own darkness." Hemcoth moved his pale head as if he were trying to shake out a memory. "Perhaps there is nothing but bones and dust in Roac but the seas around the Dead Kingdom are black and no ships enter them. Yet there are stories . . ."

"The Ships of the Dead are phantoms, to frighten children," said Mekotta firmly.

"They frighten me still," answered Hemcoth, with a half smile. "Why do you ask about the Dead Waters?"

"Because we must sail them, to reach Tir-Roac."

"No!" It was Mekotta who gasped with horror. "Prince, no. Roac is cursed. No-one can enter it."

"Lady, we were sent to Gannoth to find the way into Roac," said Kerish gently and he repeated the words of the oracle.

Hemcoth listened, white-faced. "I don't remember. I don't even know if my words are true."

"But you can guess their meaning . . ."

"Blue against black," the Prince nodded reluctantly. "The blue driftwood is not rooted in Zindar."

"And could your shipwrights make us a craft of such timber?" asked Kerish. "Is there enough?"

"Yes. But I beg you to change your mind. Princess, surely you can persuade them?"

79

"I shall be going too," said Gwerath calmly.

"Koandor," pursued Forollkin. "Do you understand that too?"

"I think that I have seen the name but I must find a much older map."

As Hemcoth searched through a chest of scrolls and Mekotta began to plead with Gwerath and Gidjabolgo, Forollkin stared down at the table. He noticed a gold framed miniature, half hidden beneath a pile of maps, and pulled it out. It showed a child with pale copper hair and brilliant green eyes.

"Who is she?"

Hemcoth returned to the table, carrying a map in a leather case.

"Princess Shameera, the younger daughter of the Queen of Seld and my betrothed."

"Betrothed? But she's too young."

"She is seven, and we will be married when she is twelve. It is the Queen's desire to marry her younger daughter to an insignificant Prince so that she will never trouble the elder."

"And why do you agree to such a marriage?" demanded Forollkin.

"How can a poor Prince of humble Gannoth refuse?" asked Hemcoth bitterly. "Her dowry will be very large."

"If Shameera is like her aunt, she will make a learned and gentle Princess for Gannoth," said Kerish.

"And if she is like her mother?"

No-one answered Gidjabolgo's question and Hemcoth slid a yellow map out of its leather case and unrolled it carefully.

"This was made before Roac fell."

The kingdom of Shubeyash was drawn in bright colours with a green and golden crown marking Tir-Roac. The citadel stood beside a small river that joined the Dirian Sea in the Bay of Koandor. Kerish frowned at the crabbed hand and then read the name aloud.

"Koandor. We must find the bay and sail up the river to Tir-Roac. Hemcoth, will you have the boat made for us, please? I cannot promise that we will be safe in Roac but we must go there and surely Zeldin will protect us."

"All of you, do all of you say the same?" asked Hemcoth.

"All of us, even the Forgite," answered Gidjabolgo dryly.

"Then I must help you," said the Prince of Gannoth, over his sister's continued protests, "but I cannot ask a subject of mine to enter the Dead Waters. Who will sail your boat?"

"I will," answered Gidjabolgo unexpectedly. "My father was a shipwright and I have often sailed small craft in the waters off Forgin."

"Elmandis be thanked," said Forollkin, "though I never thought I'd say it. You can teach me some seacraft then."

Hemcoth searched their faces for signs of fear or regret and found only anticipation.

"I had hoped your visit would be a long one," he said plaintively, "but I will order the shipwrights to begin tomorrow."

It took three weeks to fit together a boat from small pieces of blue driftwood, in the skilful Gannothan fashion. For the travellers it was a pleasant time and passed all too quickly. Gidjabolgo and Forollkin went out each day in a small fishing craft and the young Galkian learned to sail after spectacular displays of temper on both sides. Sometimes Kerish and Gwerath came with them and they all joined in torchlit hunts, when Hemcoth took his guests out on to the bay to watch his hunting gethon fly from his wrist to spear a fish on its beak.

At the end of the first week the *Zeloka* set sail for its long journey back to Galkis. Engis was unhappy at leaving them again, but Kerish watched the *Zeloka* sail with curiously little pain. He had sent messages to Kelinda but Forollkin didn't reply to his mother's letter.

As soon as the small, blue-hulled craft was ready, she was loaded with provisions and the best maps that Hemcoth could find. The white wings of a gethon were painted on her bows but Kerish named her *Starflower*. They sailed for Roac on the morning of his nineteenth birthday and Hemcoth and his sister came down to the quay to say goodbye to them.

"If we accomplish our task in Roac, we'll put in at

Losh-Sinar and send you word," promised Kerish. "From there we'll be sailing to Silnarnin."

Gidjabolgo untied the *Starflower* and bellowed orders at Forollkin.

"I wish I was coming with you," shouted Hemcoth, as they drew away from the quay, "even to the Dead Kingdom."

For a long while Kerish and Gwerath hung over the rail watching the receding island and the tiny figures of Hemcoth and Mekotta, still waving on the quay.

"I wish we were sailing across the Ocean to look for that other land," said Gwerath. "I want a journey that will never end."

Chapter 5

The Book of the Emperors: *Promises*
*"A traveller may enter no stranger realm than the mind of
another man, yet even there the star of Zeldin is constant and
shall be your guide."*

IN the morning sun the hull of the *Starflower* was a vivid
blue against the clear turquoise of the Dirian Sea. The
wind was in the west, singing its fierce cold song with the
desolate cries of the sea birds as chorus, and causing the man
hunched over the tiller to curse steadily. Nevertheless, there
was a kind of peace in Gidjabolgo's face as he steered the
boat towards Roac.

Further along the deck Forollkin reached up uncertainly
to fix a sail and shouted an order to Gwerath. She had
already done what was necessary but she nodded and
smiled. The West Wind tugged at Kerish's black and silver
hair and fluttered the pages of his book. He looked up,
roused from his placid thoughts, and noticed that his
half-brother was addressing him with some heat.

"It's all very well for you to just sit there . . ." began
Forollkin, rubbing at a calloused finger, "while the rest of
us struggle to keep this craft afloat . . ."

The Prince smiled as he closed the Book of the Emperors.

"I was charitably allowing you the pleasure of another
opportunity of shouting at me."

"I do not shout," stated Forollkin with mendacious
dignity, "but I have to make myself heard above the wind."

"You shouted at him yesterday," called Gwerath, "when
he forgot to keep hold of the rope."

"Zeldin himself would have bellowed under that
provocation!" protested Forollkin.

"I'm extremely sorry," said Kerish unconvincingly,

"but I was distracted by a shoal of Gar fish. The colours were fascinating."

"And I suppose you found it fascinating to see me knocked flat on my back by the boom?"

"It was fascinating," murmured Gwerath, "you looked so surprised."

It was said with such a straight face that it was a moment before Forollkin realized that she was teasing him.

"Well I suppose I must be pleased at giving you both such amusement!"

Kerish got up from the deck. "To show how grateful I am, I'll prepare the meal."

Forollkin snorted, "Oh, a very arduous task. Well hurry up then, I'm as hungry as a nest of Dik-birds!"

Kerish went down to their cramped cabin and through the curtains that divided it. Ducking under a hammock, he reached the chest of stores and chose some of its contents to fill four wooden bowls.

It was not long before he was back on deck but Forollkin still chose to grumble. "Even the simplest task takes you half the morning."

"I couldn't make up my mind between pickled fish and smoked cheese," answered Kerish. "The choice was too exciting."

"Oh, surely there must be some fruit left?" protested Gwerath.

"Just a little," said Kerish and surreptitiously gave her the best portion. Before putting down the last bowl he called to Gidjabolgo, "Can you come, or shall I bring yours to you?"

The wind was dropping so the Forgite lashed the tiller and sat down on a coil of rope beside Kerish.

While they ate, Forollkin struggled with a flapping chart. Finally, he knelt on the parchment and announced, "By my reckoning we're about here."

Gidjabolgo peered at the chart over Kerish's shoulder.

"Considering the curious habit you have of seeing more stars than there are in the sky, you're close to being right."

"When should we reach the Bay of Koandor?" asked Kerish quickly.

"Two to three days," answered Gidjabolgo through a

84

mouthful of cheese, "depending on the winds and allowing ample time for arguments with my Master."

"I've told you before," snapped Forollkin, "I will not have orders bellowed at me without explanation or discussion . . ."

"Forgive me, my Master, I had the idea that you'd been a soldier and would understand orders. What talkative troops you must have led, discussing each command . . ."

"In battle everything is different . . ."

"Everything is different when you're taking orders instead of giving them: playing the Fool instead of the Master . . ."

"I have been wondering," said Gwerath suddenly, "what the King of Roac could have done to destroy his people. Do you remember more than Hemcoth told us, Kerish?"

The Prince hastily joined his cousin in trying to head off another quarrel between Forollkin and the Forgite.

"Only a little. I saw his image once in Tir-Rinnon and Elmandis told me that the King of Roac cannot die, so long as he retains his key. The . . . someone else told us that King Shubeyash had stolen secrets from an ancient city that we passed the ruins of on our journey. From what we saw on Gannoth I would guess that the city was once inhabited by the creatures carved in the Cave of Pictures."

Forollkin leaned back against the boat's rail. "Well, I suppose there are things that are forbidden even to sorcerers."

"Forbidden, or merely dangerous?"

"I can't see that it matters much, Kerish; the result was destruction."

Gidjabolgo licked the last traces of fish from his bowl and said, "I find it a fascinating question. Did the sorcerer of Tir-Roac reach the natural limit of his power and walk off the edge or was he pushed by the hand that tempted him with the key?"

"I expect it's simple enough," answered Forollkin. "What moves most men to action? Greed. No doubt our sorcerer became too greedy and bit more than he could swallow."

"Greedy for what?" asked Gidjabolgo, with unusual

seriousness. "What would such a man desire?"

"Power, wealth, praise?" suggested Forollkin carelessly.

"But he was a king," said Gwerath. "He must have had all that."

"I'll swear he wanted nothing so tangible," murmured Gidjabolgo. "Power, yes. But the power of knowledge and knowledge of perfection."

"But to want those things can't be wrong!" Kerish's bright eyes transfixed the Forgite but he answered calmly.

"Why? Because you want them too?"

"Yes. Yes, I do."

"Then don't look down," said Gidjabolgo, "or you'll see how narrow the path is, and how deep the drop."

"Well, whatever the sorcerer did," exclaimed Gwerath, "I don't see why all his people should have had to suffer too."

"He was their ruler," answered Gidjabolgo. "If they didn't rebel they shared his crime."

"No, that's unjust . . ."

"I think Gidjabolgo may be right." Kerish stared out to sea watching the swooping birds. "His subjects must have had some degree of choice. If they chose to do nothing perhaps his darkness gradually filled their emptiness. Perhaps that was his unforgivable crime, the corruption of his people."

"In any case, my Mistress need not grieve," said Gidjabolgo. "The people of Roac are nothing but dust, blown about by the breath of their king."

That evening the wind freshened. Forollkin and Gidjabolgo were up for most of the night. Kerish and Gwerath slept only fitfully in their swinging hammocks. At dawn the Prince got up, took food to Gidjabolgo at the helm and persuaded Forollkin to rest for an hour or two. As he came back along the narrow deck, he saw Gwerath hanging over the rail staring down at the choppy blue-green waters. She jumped as he approached.

"Don't tell me you'd forgotten we were here? That's not easy on a boat this small," said Kerish.

"I don't know what I feel," answered Gwerath. "On the

86

plains in summer, I was used to great spaces and in the winter, to the cramped huts. But here I am in an emptiness bigger than Erandachu and yet I'm shut in with all of you, as if it were winter. Kerish, will you teach me more music?"

"Now? Yes, if that's what you really want."

"What I want is to change," said Gwerath turning to face him with her grey eyes alight. "I want to become so different that none of the Sheyasa would recognize me, not even my father."

"But change to what?"

"Forollkin has told me about the ladies of the Galkian court. I shall learn to be like them . . . You're laughing at me!"

"No. Gwerath, surely changes like that are dangerous? You start with things that are on the outside but they creep inside, deeper than you ever intended . . ."

"Oh, stop it, Kerish!" Gwerath was almost shouting at him. "Why won't you accept what I choose to say, what I choose to show? Why do you always try to get inside people?"

"Because I'm not Forollkin," said Kerish angrily, "and if you want me to treat you as shallow, perhaps you are . . . No. I don't mean that. Don't say anything. I'll get my zildar."

Gwerath found that she was shaking, but when Kerish came back on deck his face was perfectly calm. He sat down on one of the bulky coils of rope and Gwerath knelt on the deck beside him, watching his long fingers pluck out a scale. After a minute Gwerath was allowed to take the zildar into her lap and practise the same scale.

After half an hour Forollkin was back on deck again, constantly clambering past and shouting to Gidjabolgo. Their exchanges were not amiable.

"Poor Forollkin," whispered Gwerath, "how he hates taking orders from Gidjabolgo."

"Understandably," murmured Kerish, who had been deriving unworthy pleasure from this fact for some time.

"But how well he bears it," continued Gwerath warmly. "He may grumble but he carries out the orders."

"So he does." Kerish was sharply reminded of his own

behaviour under similar provocation. "Try moving your little finger up a bit."

Gwerath had almost mastered the scale when Forollkin called to them.

"Come and look at this!" He was holding one of the most precious of Hemcoth's gifts: an ebony tube fitted with a skilfully cut lens from Kolgor. The distant coastline of Roac was still no more than a shadow on the horizon but Forollkin handed the glass to Kerish and told him to look south.

The Prince held the ebony tube to his right eye. As he looked towards the coast he saw the limpid turquoise waters change to an intense and glittering black, untouched by a fleck of foam.

"The Dead Waters," said Kerish, and he gave the tube to Gwerath.

By evening they had reached the edge of the turquoise and rode at anchor in the shallow sea. The wind had dropped and both black and turquoise waters were glassy calm. That night Kerish slept badly and woke tugging at his own hands as if he were afraid of them.

At dawn the travellers ate below decks. Then Gidjabolgo went to the helm and Gwerath and the Galkians hung over the rail. They watched the *Starflower* breast the last of the sunlit turquoise waves and cleave into the black waters.

The boat shuddered as if it had struck a rock and for a heart-beat each of them listened for the sound of rending wood and water gushing into the cabin. Then the shuddering stopped, the sails billowed and the *Starflower* sailed serenely towards Roac.

"Everything's changed," whispered Gwerath, looking not at the dark sea but the pallid sky.

The customary azure had faded and the sun seemed dull and very far away. It was as if they had gone through an invisible wall into the stifling air of a long unopened room. The sea birds that had followed them from Gannoth had turned back at the edge of the Dead Waters and the slap of the waves was muted. Most disquieting of all, the West Wind was silent, but something filled the *Starflower*'s sails and thrust her forward. By afternoon they were close enough to the coast to study harsh cliffs, riven by narrow gorges that spilled black rivers into a black sea. The travellers took it in turns to use the ebony tube. Sometimes they glimpsed tall buildings on the edge of the cliffs but the land seemed to be cloaked in a deceptive haze. What at one moment appeared to be a splendid tower, at the next looked no more than a heap of stones.

Forollkin and Gwerath argued cheerfully about these mirages but to Kerish they were deeply disturbing. He turned away from the rail and the sight of Gidjabolgo crouching by the tiller moved him to fetch a cup of wine for the Forgite. Gidjabolgo drank it without a word of thanks but as Kerish sat down on the deck beside him, he murmured. "Are you so weary of the horrors of Roac that you come and look at me?"

"Familiar horrors turn into something quite different if you stare at them long enough," answered Kerish.

"Then for all our sakes, look at the cliffs again," exclaimed Gidjabolgo, "though, as they say in Forgin, you cannot outstare death."

"And what do Forgites believe concerning death?" asked Kerish.

Gidjabolgo sat back and stretched his cramped legs before he answered. "We are told that the soul lives on, tormented for a thousand years for each small sin."

"And after the torment?"

"Our teachers say that every Forgite ever born is still working out his torment, so who can tell?" Gidjabolgo shrugged. "A neat doctrine but not one that has ever influenced my conduct."

"And yet, I imagine," began Kerish cautiously, "that you have a very clear belief about what should."

"No-one has ever lived up to the standard I would set," answered Gidjabolgo, "and, before you say it, least of all myself. Knowing that, I choose to act solely for my own profit and amusement."

Kerish sat hunched up with his arms around his knees, frowning at the deck. "I wish there was only one moment of choice and that everything was over, one way or another.

I have chosen but I need help to do even the things that I desperately want."

"Yes, a clever trick is played on men. We are given a fine bow but the string is faulty and we can never reach the target unless we beg for a replacement."

Kerish didn't answer and Gidjabolgo stared at the long, downcast lashes for a while before saying, "My Master is very quiet. Have I perturbed you?"

"I was trying to imagine what it must be like to be you," said Kerish, "trying to decide whether I would think the same way as you do, if I had been born in your place, in your body . . ."

"Were you now? I have often wondered what I might have been like if I had been born the Emperor's darling."

"And would you have been like me?" Kerish had sat up straight and he waited for the answer as if it were vital to him.

"No," began Gidjabolgo slowly. "I would never . . ."

The rest of his answer was lost in the thud of Forollkin's feet as he ran towards them waving the ebony tube. Gwerath was close behind him.

"Kerish, look!"

The Prince got up to take the tube from his brother. For a few moments he looked towards the coast and then, wordlessly, he handed the tube to Gidjabolgo.

"Hemcoth said that no ships sailed these waters . . ." began Forollkin.

"Except the Ships of the Dead," murmured Kerish.

The vessel was soon visible to the naked eye and the rhythmic sweep of a double bank of oars carried it so swiftly towards the *Starflower* that there was no hope of outrunning it.

The ship of Roac shone against the liquid midnight of the Dead Waters like a gaudy mask on the face of a corpse. Every inch was gilded or limned with gem-like colours. The sails were dappled gold and amber and a dozen pennons, emblazoned with the Silver Hand of Shubeyash, flew from the triple masts.

Gidjabolgo was the first to move and within moments he was shouting orders to Forollkin. Kerish remembered the ships of Fangmere and knew that they could not long avoid being rammed. Then, if they were not killed at the first impact they might be thrown into the sea. He shuddered at the thought of the Dead Waters touching his skin, closing over his face . . . .

Gwerath's hand touched his arm. "Can you smell it?"

The silent wind carried the scent of dust and decaying timbers and a sweet odour that Kerish refused to recognize. Gwerath brushed her hands across her face as if she was trying to rub away something unclean.

Gidjabolgo pushed past them to bring the *Starflower* round and head for the pure waters of the open sea but even as the boat began to turn the shadow of the ship of Roac fell across her decks. Gwerath drew her dagger but the gesture was futile; the approaching ship could cut them in half without pausing.

Suddenly the swift, silent movement of the banks of oars stopped. Towering above the frail Gannothan craft, the ship to Roac rocked gently on the black waters. Forollkin came to his brother's side and they looked up past the still oars towards the deck.

For the first time, the Galkians saw the crew of the Ship of the Dead coming towards the rail. They moved unnaturally slowly, as if they were afraid of breaking their emaciated limbs; their garish silks hung slackly and their lank hair did not stir in the wind. A dozen faces, pale as the drowned, stared down at the travellers, but their eyes were like cracked mirrors.

To Kerish their skin seemed so white it was almost transparent but as he stared the whiteness was dimmed by the shadow of the bones beneath.

"No! Oh, Zeldin, no!" Kerish hid his face in his hands.

Suddenly the pale crew seemed to lose all interest in the travellers and they moved away from the rail like men walking against water. The long oars struck the black waves and slowly the ship turned and sailed back towards Roac.

Forollkin put an arm around Kerish. "Well it seems the Ships of the Dead won't harm us."

"I think the ship was sent to spy on us," said Kerish

shakily, "but we should follow it."

"We must. It's heading for the Bay of Koandor."

The smell of death still lingered on the wind as the *Starflower* turned again and headed for the shadowy coast of Roac.

In the Bay of Koandor the Great Harbour was filled with ships, but there was no movement on the silent quay or on the white road that wound up the cliff to the glittering walls of Tir-Roac.

The towers of the city shimmered like rainbows but in the harbour below, the ships lay rotting at their moorings. Some were half-sunk, their gilded splendour long since crumbled away, leaving only the stark outline of green timbers and a few shreds of sailcloth to wave forlornly in the silent wind.

The Ship of the Dead sailed behind a row of decaying vessels and was momentarily lost to sight in the forest of broken masts.

"But the ship must be here!" said Gwerath a few minutes later. "We followed closely; it can't have sailed out of sight so quickly!"

But there was no trace of the brilliant vessel amongst the rotting fleet.

"It could have been any of them," murmured Kerish.

"How?" demanded Forollkin. "Look, the timbers are rotten with age and the oars are broken. None of these ships will sail again."

"Unless Shubeyash moves them with his power and makes them appear almost as they must have looked before the death of Roac."

"Then those men we saw . . ." For once Forollkin was quick to understand. "But to your eyes . . . Kerish, can you bear it?"

"I shall have to," said Kerish bleakly. "Let's find the mouth of the river as quickly as we can."

For a grim hour they sailed the length of the harbour past galleons and skiffs, barges and warships, all green and rotten. Sometimes their wake, lapping against the smaller craft, was enough to sink them beneath the Dead Waters.

Two statues guarded the mouth of a river, as black as the

sea. They depicted a man with silver gloves carrying a scroll and a wand. As they passed between the statues Kerish could just recognize in the bland features the tormented face of King Shubeyash.

The *Starflower* entered a deep gorge but the silent wind was stronger than ever, billowing their sails and thrusting them deeper into Roac. On either side of the gorge, the cliffs were crowned with high green walls so they could see nothing of the vast city of Tir-Roac. Once, the gorge was spanned by a silver bridge and across it moved a slow procession of gorgeously robed children leading a blind-folded man by a halter of bells. The travellers could only wonder at the purpose of the procession as they were swept under the bridge.

Gidjabolgo tried vainly to check their speed but at sunset the wind suddenly dropped and they were able to anchor beside a marble quay at the foot of a black stair. The stair was narrow and barely seemed to lean against the cliff-face, while at its feet black fountains played.

"Well, we seem to have been brought to an entrance to Tir-Roac," said Forollkin uneasily, "but it's too late to climb the stair now. If you think this is the right place, Kerish, we'll wait here until morning."

No-one volunteered to stand guard on deck. They went down to the cabin and Forollkin bolted the hatch from below. Like all of them he was imagining what might come down the black stair in the watches of the night.

For a long time Kerish lay in his hammock too tense to fall asleep. He recited hymns and ancient prayers beneath his breath, remaining alert for the slightest noise from outside the boat.

A little after midnight he did drift into an uneasy sleep. In his dreams he saw a golden casket and knew that it contained the fifth key but the casket stood on a stone altar at the furthest end of a great cave. To reach it Kerish was forced to sidle along a narrow ledge beside a horrible chasm. He was afraid to look down and kept his hands flat against the rock, his face towards the casket.

Suddenly, the silence of the cavern was broken by a deep sigh, a sigh so desolate that he glanced round expecting the very walls to drip with tears. His startled movements dislodged a shower of pebbles. He knew at once that the creature who sighed had heard him.

A whisper came from the chasm and echoed around the cave. "*Who? Who comes at last? Who comes?*"

Spread-eagled against the rock, Kerish was silent.

"*Who comes . . . ? My key!*" The voice cracked with anger. "*You have come to steal my key! My power, my life! You shall not have it.*" The voice grew louder. "*I will take you down into my darkness.*"

From the black chasm rose two hands, whiter than the faces of the walking dead. Blindly, they groped for Kerish and the cavern was filled with desperate whispering.

"*No, my life, my key, you shall never take it!*"

Kerish knew that at the first betraying sound the hands would seize him and drag him down. Even now the long fingers were feeling their way along the rock face towards him. He clutched at the jewel at his breast and the whisper turned to a scream.

"*Light . . . give me light. Ah, pity, give me light.*"

"I can't. I can't!"

Just as the hands reached out to tear him from the ledge Kerish woke up and found that he was crying it aloud.

Within seconds, Forollkin was leaning over him and Gidjabolgo was sleepily demanding to know the danger.

"I'm sorry. I was only dreaming."

Forollkin lit one of the lamps and said, "Look, I'll leave this burning for you."

Kerish smiled his thanks and Forollkin went back to his hammock.

The others were soon asleep again but Kerish lay awake, staring at the blue flame of the lamp. His darkness was banished but he could not rid his mind of the agonized whisper, "*Ah, pity, give me light!*"

Early the next morning the four travellers left their ship and crossed the quay, skirting the silent fountains to reach the foot of the stair. Against the black water and stone, the *Starflower* glowed with the vivid colours of the world beyond Roac. In the oppressive gorge it was hard to imagine that world had ever been real.

Forollkin went first with drawn sword, Gwerath kept close to him and Kerish and Gidjabolgo walked side by side up the black steps.

Half-way up, Forollkin paused to look at a relief carved on the rock face. It showed a group of children dancing around a tall figure who stooped to embrace the smallest. The inscription was in Zindaric and Forollkin read it aloud. *"Those whom he protects by his might rejoice at the return of Shubeyash their king."*

"Do you think he can really have been popular in Roac?"

"The worst of tyrants may be the gentlest of men to those they love," said Kerish. "Perhaps Shubeyash loved his subjects."

"Or their praises," added Gidjabolgo.

The others went on but Kerish lingered in front of the trusting children and the smiling sorcerer. As he stooped to examine the lower part of the relief he noticed that the hem of his cloak was grey with dust, but there was not a speck to be seen on the polished stairs.

Even with the eyes of the Godborn he was not seeing the city as it truly was. With a pang of guilt Kerish wondered if he was simply too afraid to look at the truth.

"Kerish, don't dawdle. We must keep together."

The Prince answered his brother by hurrying up the steps.

As the travellers neared the head of the stair they saw that the high green wall that followed the edge of the cliff curved inwards in this one place. There seemed to be a gap in the wall but as Forollkin stepped on to the summit of the cliff he realized that their way was still barred. Instead of a gateway, two huge silver hands rose out of the ground and curved gracefully inwards, their fingers interlacing, to form a shining archway.

Slowly, the travellers approached the strange gateway and Forollkin marvelled to see every detail of a human hand from the pores of the skin to the ridges of the nails reproduced in burnished silver. Beyond the hands lay a courtyard paved in green and golden stone.

"Well, this is the first entrance to the city that we've

seen," began Forollkin. "Do we go through?"

Kerish hesitated. "Yes . . . but cautiously."

"Draw your weapons then," ordered Forollkin. "I'll go first."

He marched beneath the silver archway, looking ahead for any sign of danger in the courtyard. Gwerath followed at his heels, glancing from side to side.

She was the first to see the silver wrists quiver into life and bars of shadow fell across her face as the fingers flexed above her. She shouted a warning and pushed Forollkin forward. He spun round, grabbed her arm and tried to pull her clear but the fingers had caught her cloak. For a few moments Gwerath was tugged back and forwards but then she got the clasp that fastened her cloak open. The cloak slithered from her shoulders as she stumbled into the courtyard, out of reach of the silver hands. The others were not so lucky.

The fingers of the second hand had bent to enclose Gidjabolgo in a cage of flesh. He slashed at the descending hand and a liquid paler than blood gushed out to blind him. The silver palm knocked him to the ground and the fingers clenched to stop him crawling away. Kerish leapt forward and stabbed at the knuckles, exposing bone, but the hand only clenched tighter in its anger and Gidjabolgo screamed. Kerish attacked again and the thumb of the other hand jabbed towards his back to impale him on its long nail. Forollkin's sword stroke came just in time and Gwerath stood at his side stabbing at the other fingers.

Gidjabolgo screamed again. Forollkin ran round the clenched hand, ducked under the arched wrist and drove his sword upwards. He severed the artery and pale blood spurted out. The fingers twitched wildly and Kerish dragged Gidjabolgo out from under them. Gwerath thrust again at the other hand and leaped back as it tried to crush her between thumb and finger. Kerish and Gidjabolgo were already clear. Forollkin tugged out his sword and the hand above him suddenly went limp. Gwerath pulled him away from its cold flesh as the other hand stretched towards them, straining to break free of the stones that trapped it at the wrist. The fingers sidled to and fro, like a giant silver

96

spider and, finding Gwerath's cloak, tore it to pieces with mindless fury.

At a safe distance, Gidjabolgo sat gasping on the green pavement. He was badly bruised, but no bones were broken and Kerish and Gwerath were shaken but unharmed. Forollkin unwound the sash at his waist and used it to wipe the pale blood from his face and hair. There was nothing he could do about his sodden clothes.

"Well now we know never to trust a sorcerer's handclasp," panted Gidjabolgo

When they had all recovered their breath they looked around them.

A high green wall, broken by six slender towers, enclosed the square. From the parapet of each tower flew a standard, embroidered with the Silver Hands of Shubeyash. The same device was carved on the pillars flanking the entrance to a broad street that led into the city. Grouped around one of the pillars were four stone-masons. Their eyes were like pebbles smoothed by the sea and they struck silent blows with the mallets in their clenched hands.

Approaching cautiously, the travellers saw that the masons were altering the blazon of Shubeyash. Above the Silver Hands, two eyes had been added and between them, only half-carved, was a third.

Gidjabolgo nodded towards the street.

"Do we follow that?"

"We must find the Palace of Shubeyash," said Kerish. "The casket will be there."

"If we climbed one of those towers, we could get a good view of the city," suggested Forollkin.

"True, but let me go alone," answered Kerish. "Remember the Ship of the Dead. We can't be certain how ruinous these towers really are."

"What . . . ? Oh, I see." Forollkin absorbed this disquieting idea with a visible effort. "Well it looks like hard stone; there's no reason why it shouldn't last for centuries. We'll both go up."

"If the steps are unsafe, I'm lighter . . ." began Gwerath and then checked herself, "but I'll stay and guard the foot of the stair."

Forollkin thanked her with an approving smile and he and Kerish cautiously climbed the spiral staircase inside the green tower. They stepped out on to the parapet, avoiding the gleaming banner, and looked out over Tir-Roac.

Spread before them were ornate towers and fantastic domes, gleaming with amber and amethyst, roofed with silver and linked by bridges slung from golden chains. The squares were paved with marble and full of statues and fountains. There were no gardens and the slow, silent figures of the dead walked the shining streets.

Kerish and Forollkin saw that the road beginning in the courtyard below led straight towards a building that towered above the city in the shape of a crown. The outer wall was of translucent crystal patterned with vast silver hands and through it glowed the rich emerald of the inner wall.

Forollkin was still staring at the Palace of Shubeyash when Kerish nudged him and pointed southwards. Only a short way from the Palace, the city seemed infected by a leprous growth of ruin and darkness. Even as they looked, shadows everywhere encroached on the brightness.

Slowly the brothers descended the stair to tell the others what they had seen. With drawn swords they edged past the silent masons, who were still intent on carving the third eye, and entered the city of Shubeyash.

Chapter 6

The Book of the Emperors: *Sorrows*
But the young Prince said: "I will not rejoice in my death,"
and he denied the way of Zeldin and of Imarko his
Foremother. "I shall stretch out my arms, not to embrace the
darkness but to hold it back, until the end of my strength. Only
beasts crawl into the shadows and wait for death. I am a man,
and I defy Her!" But the Emperor said to him: "Oh, my
child, fight with your body, but in your mind let go of life
while it is still precious to you. Then it will be your servant
and bring you joy. Those that cling to life crush what they
hold most dear and nothing but dust remains."

THE street was paved in cloudy amethyst and lined with slender trees, carved in ivory with scarlet gems for blossoms. To either side rose houses shrieking their ugly wealth with every gilded door, every rare shell pressed into the painted walls, every glittering statue.

At the upper windows sat women of high rank, their shaven heads covered with nets of pearls, their hands encased in cages of filigree so that they could do nothing for themselves. The travellers stared up at a woman seated in an ebony chair, opening and closing her pale lips, while servants fed her from a silver dish.

The way narrowed and Forollkin backed hurriedly to avoid a procession that had issued silently from a side street. The travellers watched it pass from amongst the ivory trees.

First walked three slaves ringing mute bells and behind them marched a group of free citizens in green and sable mantles. Their lips moved as if they were shouting and in their midst a young child was carried in an ivory chair. The men on either side of him had seized his wrists and spread out the small hands to show that the little fingers of both

99

had been recently severed. Tears of pain still disfigured the child's face. Kerish noticed with a shiver of disgust that all the men lacked one or more fingers on each hand and guessed that it was some mark of rank or office.

Grimly, Forollkin led them on and the soft echo of their footsteps brought a white face to each dark window. They hurried beneath an archway into a street lined with colossal statues of Shubeyash holding out his gloved hands to the tiny figures of citizens clustered at his feet.

"Hands," thought Kerish. "Always hands. Hands clinging to life and causing death." The image of the white hands of his dream rose from their chasm to clutch at his calm. He felt in his tunic for the Jewel of Zeldin, remembering the darkened glass in the chamber of Elmandis and the face he had seen in its depths.

"It will draw him to you." Elmandis and Saroc had both warned him and even as he clutched the jewel, Kerish sensed a surge of power trying to reach him. Though he still saw the illusory spendours of Tir-Roac, Kerish understood now that the whole city was like a body to the dead sorcerer, a body which he strove to animate.

As the Prince looked at the statue above him, its marble seemed to blanch and soften into skin, the stiff limbs grew supple, the feet moved a fraction on the pedestal . . .

"No!" Kerish closed his eyes and thought of stone in all its black smoothness, its cool hardness. Stone: solid, ageless, a prison that could not be broken.

"Kerish, what is it? You're trembling. Is there danger?" The Prince laid his hand on the black marble. "Not now."

Against the last statue in the street, scaffolding had been set up and masons were splintering the stone with silent blows, re-carving the face of Shubeyash. The travellers hurried past and down a flight of shallow steps that led into a huge square, filled with people.

In the centre stood another tall statue of Shubeyash, garlanded with flowers. Forollkin fancied that there was something wrong about its face, some curious deformity and he was glad he wasn't close enough to see it clearly. All around the base of the statue, women were dancing. They were naked, except for ropes of coral, their smiles seemed nailed to their faces and their hands were caged.

Hundreds of citizens stood motionless, with their eyes towards the dancers. To cross the square the travellers would have to move among them.

"I can't," whispered the Prince.

For a few seconds, as he looked across the square, Kerish saw brittle bones, half covered by scraps of flesh and decaying rags, standing upright or moving in a slow tortured dance. He shut his eyes and sat down on the steps, trying not to be sick.

"I would not exchange your eyes for mine," said Gidjabolgo as Kerish fought to conjure pleasant images to banish the sight of death. He couldn't do it. Tir-Roac was too strong.

Forollkin bent anxiously over him but it was Gwerath that Kerish called to his side.

"Gwerath, will you close your eyes and take my hand and think of the most beautiful place you can remember or imagine?"

"But why?"

"I need to see through your eyes," said Kerish. "Please, Gwerath, think of a place and think of yourself there and put us beside you. Think of your place, think of the sounds you would hear, the scents you would smell, the feel of the earth beneath your feet. Try, Gwerath, and you can help us all!"

Gwerath took her cousin's shaking hands and obediently closed her eyes. Her thoughts were clouded at first with the darkness of Tir-Roac but gradually the picture in her head grew stronger and clearer. Kerish saw it in his mind's eye in a dazzle of light as if he was looking into the sun.

The Princess of the Sheyasa had pictured herself walking barefoot, amongst lush grass and nodding windflowers whose pungent scent filled the air. Watch trees sprang up from these plains and in the distance a turquoise sea beat on a white shore. In that place Gwerath wore a dress of roseate silk but her dagger still hung at her waist and her silver hair flowed loose. Beside her walked Forollkin with one arm around her waist. The Prince and Gidjabolgo were blurs of colour beside the sharp images of Gwerath and Forollkin.

Kerish sat for a long time, absorbing the calm of Gwerath's vision. The others saw nothing, but Gidjabolgo thought he recognized the scent of windflowers. Finally, Kerish stood up, still holding Gwerath by the right hand.

"Keep your eyes closed," he murmured. "We'll lead you across." He took her down the last few steps with the others only a pace behind.

Fixing his eyes on the ground, Kerish wove his way through the silent crowd, taking infinite care not even to brush against the green and sable cloaks. He froze once as a ripple of movement passed through the crowd. A dance was over and the citizens clapped their mutilated hands in silent applause.

Kerish knew that Shubeyash watched their progress across the square. One after another the dead would turn and stare and Shubeyash looked out through their eyes like a creature trapped behind a window, desperately trying to break the glass.

Approaching the central statue now were a group of young men. One of them brandished a knife and slashed at his left hand. Blood spurted out, two severed fingers fell and the crowd applauded. As their mouths moved Kerish heard the faintest of whispers, *"Shubeyash! Long live Shubeyash!"*

He closed his eyes for a moment, and watched Gwerath stoop to pick a windflower. With the sound of her sea in his ears he opened his eyes again and walked on.

They were almost across the square when Kerish was forced to lead his companions through a narrow gap between three hooded soldiers and a group of women. He walked stealthily behind the women, so close that he could see every seed pearl on their diadems, every coil of hair. Then one of them turned.

He choked at her carrion breath and flinched from the wild eyes in the naked skull.

The sudden cruel pressure of Kerish's hand broke Gwerath's vision. Her eyes flew open and Kerish started into a run. For a minute the others ran with him until he sank down on to a low wall and buried his head in his hands.

After a moment he looked up. "Gwerath, I couldn't have crossed that square without you."

"And you?" Gwerath turned eagerly to Forollkin. "Did I help you too?"

"Well I didn't see anything but the square and the people, but if you've helped Kerish, you've helped our quest. I said once that you couldn't. I know now that I was wrong."

"We must hurry," broke in Kerish sharply.

"Why?" demanded Gidjabolgo. "Do beasts hurry into a trap? This sorcerer lets us walk his streets for his own purpose not ours."

"Kerish, do you think that's true?" asked Forollkin.

"Yes," said Kerish as a woman, awkwardly holding a baby to her breast with her caged hands, came out on to a balcony and stared down at them.

"Yes. He watches us always and I can feel him drawing us to the centre of Tir-Roac."

"But why should he want us to go to his Palace?" asked Gwerath. "Why not kill us here, if he's so powerful?"

Kerish fingered the Jewel of Zeldin as he spoke.

"There is something he wants of me. He also fears us and wishes to destroy us, but desire is struggling with fear. We must go on."

"Look at me, Kerish," ordered his brother. "Do you really think we should walk straight into the Palace? Are you sure that the sorcerer hasn't somehow influenced you? Surely we should fight rather than let ourselves be dragged towards him?"

"I'm not sure, but I feel that we must reach the heart of this darkness. Shubeyash is most vulnerable there."

"Not more powerful still?" Forollkin hesitated. "Well, I've been wrong before in not trusting your understanding of sorcerers. We'll do as you say."

"Zeldin let me be right," thought Kerish as he clasped his brother's hand.

As they stepped on to the street again, he felt that the city had trembled and for a moment the colours dimmed and the shadows lengthened.

They walked on quickly, until forced back into the doorway of a house by the approach of four slaves carrying a palanquin hung with almond silk. Inside lay a woman whose lustrous hair streamed over the cushions. She wore a circlet of silver hands and pearl-sewn gauzes that barely concealed her body, but the impression of beauty was destroyed by the horror of her blanched face and soulless gaze. Each stiff movement emphasized the living death beneath the alabaster skin and the scents that lingered about her no longer came from the flowers in her caged hands.

Kerish wondered if she had been some cherished queen or concubine. How could the sorcerer bear to look at her ruined loveliness? Surely it was better to let the body decay and keep only the memory? But this sorcerer could not die and perhaps in the agony of his loneliness even these grotesque shadows were better than dust and darkness.

"Shubeyash," whispered Kerish, "I'm coming."

For an hour they walked along the Royal Road towards the Palace, watched from dark casements and by the silent processions whose destinations had long since fallen into dust. Sometimes, looking back, the travellers saw the brightness fade and darkness encroaching on areas of the city they had just passed through.

Finally, they approached the outer wall of the Palace and an archway in the crystal. Masked soldiers stood on either side of it, holding barbed spears. As the travellers moved towards them, they bowed and thrust the points of their spears into the ground.

"Zeldin," whispered Forollkin as he passed between the guards, "I think I'd prefer a knife in the back to this sorcerer's welcome!"

They paused for a minute between the outer and inner walls to stare at the patterned crystal and the glowing emerald stone. But after a few moments the colours seemed to dim before their eyes and cracks appeared in the crystal as if Shubeyash was too weary to preserve the glory of his citadel for long.

Beyond an archway in the emerald wall stretched a long passage hung with tapestries, each woven from feathers torn from the breasts of a thousand birds. Twelve ivory doors led off the passageway and between each of them stood a sable-cloaked sentry, carrying an axe and a silver knife.

To Kerish, these surroundings seemed almost familiar and he knew as they approached a flight of emerald steps that these led to the throne-room of Shubeyash. Torches gave a flickering light but no warmth and Kerish was shivering. *"Thief."* Kerish heard a voice like dust. *"Thief, come close so I may kill you. The key is mine for ever, the key and the darkness."*

The others followed Kerish up the steps and they found themselves in a pillared gallery. Below, lit by jewelled globes that hung upon the air, lay the throne-room of Shubeyash. The ivory throne of the Kings of Roac stood on a dais and from its footstool stretched a silver grille that spanned the hall. The grille was fixed four feet above the floor of the hall so that no-one could stand upright in the sorcerer's presence.

The travellers saw courtiers old and young, dragging themselves on their bellies towards the dais. Their ashen faces, staring up through the grille, were lit by the harsh glare of the hovering globes, but Shubeyash was swathed in shadow. Kerish could only make out a frail figure in a green mantle whose hands were hidden by silver gloves, the ancient insignia of the Kings of Roac.

Then the Prince shrank back against a pillar as the sorcerer turned his head and looked up towards the gallery. He looked, not with his eyes, but with his mind, for the face of Shubeyash had been shattered by some terrible blow.

Kerish sensed his own horror mirrored in the sorcerer and felt Shubeyash withdrawing power from Roac to restore his broken body. The globes flickered and for a few seconds the travellers saw the throne-room desolate and ruined. The silver grille had collapsed with a dozen pathetic skeletons crushed beneath it and the pale face of Shubeyash shone against the growing dark. Then the last light went out.

The travellers stood, huddled together, in the gallery until Kerish whispered, "He is coming."

"How can you know?" Gwerath's voice was edged with panic.

"I can see him," murmured Kerish. "As though he were

105

painted on my eyes. He is thinking of me and moving through the dark very slowly. Can't you hear him?"

"Come. I knew that you must come. He warned me but you shan't take my key. Come close so my silver hands can reach you!"

Kerish winced at the malignance behind the words, but the Lord of Tir-Roac had no tongue. He spoke only to the mind and the others heard nothing.

"Do we stay here?" asked Forollkin anxiously.

"Yes. No, wait . . ." Kerish focused all his thoughts on Shubeyash, forcing himself to look at the ruined body that now crawled up a winding stair; to look at the white face, savagely divided by a line of shadow between the desperate eyes.

The sorcerer spoke continually, more to himself than his enemy. *"Thief, cruel thief, you would take my life. But I will cling, I will never let go. The key is hidden, he will never find it. I will never let it go, never, or I am lost."*

Kerish saw and felt each step. The stones were dank and cold and the torches gave no light.

"Light, I must have light. Light to show the Seldian tapestry with the dancing queens, dancing into dust . . . dust. No! It hangs there still. I can see it. I can make them see it but the pain of it, the pain . . ."

It was agony to cling to his body but he would not let go.

"Hands," murmured Kerish. "There are hands inside my gloves. I won't let go. I am more than shadow. Give me light!"

"Kerish!" Forollkin shook his brother by the shoulders.

The Prince stopped moaning and stretched out his hands, staring at the splayed fingers.

"Kerish, what is it?"

"I know now," he said softly. "When I . . . when he thought of it, I saw."

"Thought of what?" Forollkin tried to speak calmly and drive away the grotesque fear that it was not his brother who stood beside him in the darkness.

"The casket," answered Kerish. "When he thought of the key he pictured the treasure chamber. I know where it is. Shubeyash moves towards that chamber but he is slow and we might reach it first."

Kerish left the gallery, moving swiftly down a passage to his left. He needed no light to guide him but the others couldn't follow. For them the darkness was total.

Gwerath stumbled over something and cried, "Kerish, please wait!"

"We are not worms to tunnel in the dark," growled Gidjabolgo.

For a moment their voices severed the Prince's link with Shubeyash.

"I'm sorry," he whispered.

"We need a light," said Forollkin.

Reluctantly, Kerish drew out the Jewel of Zeldin and held it high. The white flame seemed to burn deep within the purple gem but at once the corridor was faintly lit. Gwerath saw that she had stumbled on the bones of a child; a page perhaps at the court of Shubeyash.

"We must hurry," said Kerish.

Almost gladly he returned to the dark embrace of the mind of Shubeyash and led his companions along twisting passages, down a flight of steps and into a hall filled with statues of the sorcerer. Beyond were tarnished silver doors with two heaps of bone and rusted mail close by, where sentries had once stood.

The travellers stepped carefully between them and Kerish pushed open the doors. By the light of the Jewel of Zeldin they saw a huge chamber crowded with iron-bound chests. The wood had rotted away and dusty treasures spilled out on to the floor. But high on an altar of green stone a golden casket still shone brightly. Kerish felt for the keys at his waist and then gasped with pain as the Jewel of Zeldin seared his hand.

A door at the far end of the treasure chamber swung slowly open. Torches leapt into life on the walls and decay was banished by their pale light. The treasure chests stood whole on the polished floor but the travellers looked only at Shubeyash.

The King of Roac stood before them. His face was cruelly marred but his eyes were filled with life and they burned with a terrible intensity.

To Kerish they seemed more pitiable than the soulless

eyes of his subjects. Only the bodies of the people of Roac had been forced into a mockery of life. This was a chained spirit.

"My Lord," said Kerish gently, "I have come for the key to your prison. Surrender it to me and I will release you."

"Thief, liar!"

The tongueless words of Shubeyash shuddered through the chamber. *"You have seen the glory of my kingdom, which shall endure for ever, but you will die for your trespass."*

"The splendour is gone, Shubeyash. Your kingdom is dust."

"No! You have seen my subjects; I have given them immortality."

"You gave them nothing but death." Kerish looked beyond Shubeyash to the golden casket. "Nothing remains. They are gone from you."

"They are here!" The voice of Shubeyash was heavy with pain. *"They answer to my summons. Look!"*

Kerish turned to see the two sentries entering the treasure chamber. He spoke quickly to the others.

"Close your eyes and keep them closed whatever you hear or feel. Think of everything you love. I need your strength!"

As they obeyed, the sorcerer stepped forward, raising his gloved hands to shield his face from the light of the Jewel of Zeldin.

"You cannot escape me so. I will enter your thoughts and join them to my kingdom. Even the memory of all things beautiful and beloved I can destroy, for I am Shubeyash, greatest of sorcerers!"

The outline of the sorcerer's hands flickered against the wall and the crooked fingers seemed to form a cage of shadows around Kerish. The sentries stood on either side of him, staring with helpless eyes. Their spears pointing at his heart.

"Zeldin aid me," murmured Kerish and the jewel glowed in his hand, but the brightness failed to reach the sorcerer. The King of Roac stood half in shadow, half in the unnatural glare of the torches of illusion.

"Shubeyash," pleaded the Prince, "I have come to banish your darkness and free you from your loneliness."

"No, you come to steal my immortality."

The scarlet threads of madness glittered against the blackness of his fury and Kerish despaired. The sorcerer whispered of torture and death and for an anguished moment Kerish thought of what his failure must mean for Forollkin and Gwerath and Gidjabolgo. But even as his mind shaped their names he felt their presence, felt that he could lean on their strength and trust them not to let him fall. His hand clenched on the jewel and he looked steadily into the face of Shubeyash.

"My Lord of Roac, you called me here, but now I summon you. Come to me, come closer!"

The blackness between the desperate eyes sickened him but Kerish held out his right hand to Shubeyash.

"Come to me, I offer you peace."

The sorcerer dragged his broken body slowly forward but his mind leapt before it.

Kerish cowered before the onslaught of dark images. Severed and bleeding hands caressed him, dark wings enfolded and stifled him, flames caught at his cloak, dead lips kissed his cheek. In his torment Kerish struggled to think of Forollkin's strong embrace, of Gwerath walking among windflowers, of Gidjabolgo bent over his zildar, of the Emperor in his garden and the calm face of Izeldon.

"No! You shall not have them!"

The comforting images were shattered.

"You are alone and you will die alone."

"No, Shubeyash, I have accepted love and given it. I cannot die alone, but you . . . You are trapped within yourself, only you can know such loneliness."

"I rule Roac," whispered Tir-Roac's king. *"My subjects love and worship me!"*

"You have no subjects. Look at them, Shubeyash, look!"

With the eyes of the Godborn, Kerish stared fiercely at the silent sentries and the skulls gleamed through their withered flesh.

"They are dead, all dead. You have power over nothing but bones and dust. Let go!"

The white fire of the Jewel of Zeldin blazed with renewed splendour. The sorcerer took one step forward but still he shielded his face.

"It burns. I cannot bear it. You mean to kill me with your light but I will destroy you first."

Kerish's hand seemed almost transparent as the light flowed through it but he could not hold back the darkness of Shubeyash.

The floor split open at his feet. He stood again on the brink of the chasm and the white hands rose to drag him down. The fingers caught at his cloak as the shadow spread across the face of Shubeyash, destroying every feature.

"We will fall together!"

"No!" The jewel blazed in Kerish's hand and the pain was more terrible than the darkness of Shubeyash, but in a second he would fall.

"Zeldin, Zeldin, help me, save us from the dark. Give us light!"

Hands closed on Kerish, and the Jewel of Zeldin shattered. The light was released and the sorcerer screamed in desperate agony. For a second Kerish saw his own fingers black against the brilliance and then the light engulfed Shubeyash.

The illusory flesh was scorched away. Nothing remained but bone and a high, terrible screaming. Then Kerish, too, was screaming, his eyes ravaged by the brilliance. White flames thrust through his skin, filling his body, dissolving the very bones. He was burning alive and he was blind. The light had grown too bright for him to see and nothing else remained in his universe.

"Shubeyash." Kerish tried to speak but he had no lips. They were gone, consumed by fire and soon the flames would reach his heart. He ceased to struggle against the annihilation; the pain increased and passed beyond his power to feel, as a fierce joy matched his agony.

Slowly the screams faded leaving only a deep sigh, and a dying whisper. *"Take it. Let me go."*

The light no longer seemed white: it was filled with colours he had never before perceived. They moved in patterns that unfolded too quickly, or perhaps, too slowly, for his comprehension. All that had ever oppressed him was stripped away. He was free and in a moment he would see

110

the whole that he was part of. Before that moment came the light dimmed to a gentle darkness and he was not afraid as he sank down into it, only sad. He knew that something he had always wanted had been just within his grasp: now it was as far away as ever.

Slowly he became aware of his body and the tears stinging his face.

"Kerish?"

He realized that he was lying on the ground with his head in someone's lap.

"I can't see."

His own voice sounded harsh to him.

"Don't worry, we couldn't either at first," said Forollkin. "It passes off, but your hand . . ."

"What's wrong?" Kerish flexed his right hand, but the left he could not feel at all. He struggled to sit up and the darkness faded into the pale light of dawn streaming through the broken roof of the ruined chamber.

Forollkin and Gwerath were kneeling by him and Gidjabolgo stood scowling behind them. All three seemed absurdly anxious.

"Shubeyash?"

"He is gone," said Gwerath.

Then Kerish saw the silver gloves lying amongst a heap of bones. Partial memory returned.

"The Jewel of Zeldin." Kerish looked down at his left hand and at the fingers curved as if they still held their treasure. The jewel was gone without trace and he could not move his hand.

"Does it hurt?" asked Gwerath.

"No. I can't even feel you touching it."

With his other hand, he fumbled for the keys at his waist. Forollkin helped him up and Gidjabolgo held the casket steady for him to unlock. Inside lay a slender key, set with a black gem.

"He surrendered it finally," murmured Kerish. "I didn't have to steal it."

"What happened?" asked Forollkin. "I knew the sentries were close and I could just hear the sorcerer's voice and yours. I remembered what you said. I kept my eyes closed and thought about Galkis and of . . . of other beautiful things. Then I heard something shatter. I opened my eyes. There was a flash of light and when I could see again Shubeyash and all his illusions were gone."

"It wasn't just light," cried Gwerath, "there was a sound too. It was beautiful but it hurt me."

"It began like music," muttered Gidjabolgo.

"You heard no screams?" asked Kerish.

The others shook their heads and into the uneasy silence Forollkin said, "For Zeldin's sake, our work here's done. Let's get out of Roac."

"There is nothing to hurt us now," murmured Kerish. "In time, even the legends will die."

As Forollkin helped him to fit the fifth key on the golden chain, Gidjabolgo picked up the cloven skull of Shubeyash.

"I thought the sorcerers of Zindar were all human once."

"So they were, all seven," answered Kerish.

"Well this is surely not the skull of a man," said Gidjabolgo. "Here, where the blow fell, this looks like the socket of a third eye."

"Imarko protect us. Put it down!" Forollkin shuddered. "Do you feel strong enough to move, Kerish? We can see to your hand on the *Starflower*."

The Prince nodded and they walked back through the ruined palace. Everywhere among the broken splendours lay the dead but the West Wind now came shrieking in, stirring the rags that clung to the cold bones and shifting dust to cover them at last.

The walls of emerald stone still stood but the crystal lay in a million shards, sparkling in the sunlight. As they crossed the great courtyard, they heard the cries of sea-birds and saw them wheeling against a sky of deepening blue. One of them flew down to perch on a crumbling statue of the sorcerer king and preen its feathers. Kerish knew that Tir-Roac was finally dead and now life could return

Chapter 7

The Book of the Emperors: *Warnings*
And because the High Priest counselled prudence, the young
Emperor cried out against him: "Must I bend with every wind
that blows and never stand against the storm?" Then the High
Priest answered him: "To many of the lesser winds you must
bow for the sake of those who shelter beneath you but there are
great storms loosed on the world against which every man must
stand, though they will surely break him." "But how may I
recognize such storms? How may I know?" The High Priest
could not answer his Emperor.

DWARFED by quinqueremes of Chiraz, the *Starflower*
sheltered from the first gales of autumn in the harbour
of Losh-Sinar among the skiffs and pleasure barges.
Gwerath stood on deck watching merchants bargaining for
perfumes and poisons, while warriors from the Five
Kingdoms stared at delicate Loshites who hid their painted
faces behind fans of lace and ivory.

Forollkin had gone ashore to buy provisions. He had
refused to let Kerish or Gwerath come with him and
declined, with much embarrassment, to say why. Gidjabolgo had also slipped ashore, leaving Kerish to guard
the boat as best he could with one hand still paralyzed.

Behind the warehouses that flanked the quay rose the
famous inns and pleasure gardens of Losh; above them the
sombre faceless houses of the Loshites and the temple of
their nameless god.

A ship from Proy docked beside the *Starflower* and emaciated slaves with the marks of floggings across their backs
unloaded chests of precious irivanee. As merchants rushed
forward to bid for stones of the deepest purple, Kerish

thought guiltily of the irivanee set in his zeloka jewels. The slave quarries of Proy were the ugly price for their beauty.

Gwerath wrinkled her nose as the reek of strong scents drifted over from a group of Loshites in diaphanous robes of coral silk, sewn with jangling discs of pearl. Incongruously, the squat figure of Gidjabolgo was moving amongst them. One of the Loshites spoke to the Forgite from behind his fan but Gidjabolgo shook his head and hurried towards the boat. Gwerath saw that his arms were full of fresh fruit.

"They'll charge you the price of a pearl for the dirt beneath your feet in this town," growled Gidjabolgo, as he climbed aboard and tossed down the scarlet and saffron fruits. "We might as well dine on these. I fancy our gallant Captain has fallen victim to one of the famous distractions of Losh. He won't be back before nightfall."

"It will take time to bargain for all the provisions we need," said Gwerath, choosing a ripe yellow fruit and biting into it.

"Who am I to question the worldly wisdom of my Mistress?" answered Gidjabolgo, as he peeled and quartered fruit for Kerish who accepted it gratefully.

"Gidjabolgo, you're a paragon. Do you know, it's only in the past week that I've discovered quite how much I hate fish."

"And smoked cheese," put in Gwerath.

They had had few provisions left for the voyage from Tir-Roac to Losh-Sinar and for the last week they had lived on raw fish, scraps of cheese and mouldering bread. They ate for a while in greedy silence and then Gwerath glanced up at a group of crop-headed warriors from Soraz, with snake-skin cloaks and long, curved swords.

"If all you say about the Five Kingdoms is true, Kerish, why haven't they gobbled up a rich place like Losh?"

It was Gidjabolgo who spat out a mouthful of pips and answered. "The Loshites fear their neighbours but they live by pleasing them. They pay tribute in delicate pleasures and even the barbarians know that if you pick a flower, you kill it."

"But aren't the men of Losh ashamed to dress like wo—

114

men and bow and cringe to please barbarians?"

"They have more than that to be ashamed of, Mistress, but they shut off the dark part of their lives," said Gidjabolgo, "and pretend it isn't there. Among themselves they are as strict as any Priest of Dard. A Loshite would lose his hand for so much as brushing against one of his own women, but with strangers he may do whatever is profitable and count it service to his country."

"But how can they endure such divided lives?"demanded Gwerath, blushing slightly.

"Such contradictions are not uncommon. Though perhaps my Mistress is too young to have noticed them."

"Well if they are common, they shouldn't be!" declared Gwerath fiercely. "Kerish, surely you agree?"

The Prince had been staring down at his wounded hand.

"I think so, but I'm not sure. The Loshites are a gentle people."

Gwerath's fierceness melted into concern. "Cousin, you look ill. Is your hand hurting you?"

"Sometimes it burns and the feeling comes back briefly, but I still can't move it."

Abruptly, he got up and went below to lie in his hammock, silent but not asleep.

On the deck, Gwerath and Gidjabolgo were equally silent as they watched the crowded quay and waited for Forollkin.

He finally returned at dusk, followed by several porters carrying baskets of food and a barrel of wine.

Gwerath didn't leave her seat astride the rail but she shouted, "Why have you been so long? Kerish was worried about you."

Forollkin continued to give orders and it was not until he had paid off the last of the porters that he answered her question.

"It takes time to find the best provisions and bargain for them. Then I had to search out a ship to take our letters to Hemcoth and Mekotta, and discover who was the best physician in the city. I'll take Kerish to him tomorrow."

The Prince had overheard as he came back on deck. "Thank you, but I don't need a physician."

Gidjabolgo strolled round the deck. "Well, we mustn't chide our Captain for being late, no doubt he wanted to see the sights of the city."

Forollkin didn't answer him directly. "I've brought some roast fowls from an inn, so we'd better eat them before they get cold."

Gidjabolgo pounced on a basket, already damp with grease, and Gwerath hurriedly fetched platters and knives from the cabin.

As they knelt in a circle to share out the food, Forollkin suddenly delved in the pouch at his waist.

"Gwerath, that hair of yours is always getting in the way."

Startled, Gwerath pushed back the silver mass with greasy fingers. Forollkin drew out a somewhat crumpled scarf of lavender silk embroidered with crystal beads.

"I thought you needed something to tie it back."

Gwerath hastily rubbed her hands on her leather tunic and took the scarf. Her fingers explored the softness of the silk and the shape of the beads, but her eyes were on Forollkin. He cut short her thanks and avoided his brother's penetrating gaze.

"Well, shall we start? I thought you'd all be ravenous."

They sailed from Losh-Sinar just after dawn. Kerish had again refused to see a physician and Forollkin did not seem anxious to linger amongst the pleasures of Losh. After studying Hemcoth's charts, Gidjabolgo plotted a course that would take them through the Straits of Proy, across open sea to avoid coming too close to the inhabited coast of Chiraz, till they neared the Mountains of Chire.

The Straits of Proy were crowded with merchant vessels and pleasure craft but as the *Starflower* sailed westwards they entered lonelier waters.

For the first four days the weather was good and they had a following wind but on the fifth morning the *Starflower* ran into a storm.

Forollkin and Gidjabolgo worked unceasingly to keep the boat afloat, till their hands were raw and they were too exhausted even to sleep. Gwerath and Kerish helped when they could. Gidjabolgo insisted that they all worked roped

116

to the ship's rail, a precaution that saved Gwerath's life when she was knocked down and washed overboard by the fierce slap of a wave.

After two days the storms eased. Gidjabolgo lashed the tiller and curled up beside it, while Forollkin forced the others to strip off their sodden clothes before collapsing into their hammocks.

Gidjabolgo was the first to wake and by the light of a new dawn, he saw that the storm winds had blown them far along their course and the Mountains of Chire already overwhelmed the distance. After their first uninterrupted meal for several days, the *Starflower* limped towards the lonely coast of western Chiraz.

Late that afternoon, they put in at a small, deserted cove to refill their water barrels at a stream chattering down from the mountains. All four of them went ashore and Forollkin returned from a hunt with two plump birds and an unknown animal, which tasted delicious roasted by Gidjabolgo over a driftwood fire.

As they sat on a grassy slope overlooking the pebbled beach, the warmth of summer seemed to linger in the autumn air. Kerish could hardly believe that this quiet place was part of the Five Kingdoms that threatened Galkis, the kingdoms they had been brought up to mistrust and fear.

Forollkin was talking about Galkis and Gwerath was teasing him by refusing to believe his descriptions of the Golden City.

"It's all true. I'm no legend weaver!" protested Forollkin." For that you have to go to Kerish."

The Prince was lying on his back in the soft grass frowning at the stars. He didn't appear to be listening but he turned his head when Gidjabolgo spoke.

"I'm told that in Galkis, sunset is the time for singing. Shall I play for you?" His plump hands caressed the Prince's zildar that he had brought ashore from the boat.

Kerish nodded. "Someone should play it now that I can't. It wasn't made for silence."

Nevertheless he didn't listen to the rippling notes for long.

"Gidjabolgo," he asked softly, "why didn't you become

117

a shipwright like your father?"

"He early recognized my rare qualities and had me taught to sing and play and caper," answered the Forgite. "The life of a hired grotesque is more profitable than that of a shipwright and he had other sons."

"But surely you can't have wanted such a life?"

"Why not, my Prince? A master pleased with a cruel jest at someone else's expense will toss his Fool more than a craftsman earns in half a year."

"But you hate servitude," persisted Kerish. "You've never tried to hide it."

Gidjabolgo fingered the gilded head that crowned the Prince's zildar. "Perhaps I preferred to dwell among the books and music and treasures of a merchant's mansion instead of the ugliness of a shipwright's hut. Not only the Godborn have eyes and ears to satisfy."

Kerish sat up. "I see, and I who have so many treasures have never given you anything. What can I give you, Gidjabolgo? This bracelet?"

He plucked awkwardly at the crimson beads at his wrist but the Forgite laughed. "On my wrist it would lose its charm. Leave your bracelet where it is and I'll look at it; but when the quest is over, I shall claim my servant's wages."

"Kerish," called Gwerath, from a little way down the slope, "Forollkin has been telling me about temple actors and their plays. Will you sing us a song from one of them?"

The firelight enriched the gold of Gwerath's skin and glittered on the crystal embroidery of the scarf binding back her hair.

Kerish smiled. "Gladly. I'll sing you 'The Wise Prince'. The words are in High Galkian but I'll translate afterwards."

Kerish sang a long, unaccompanied account of the life of Jezreen-lo-Kaash, younger son of the Twelfth Emperor. When it was over, he explained to Gwerath how Prince Jezreen had left his father's court and wandered through Galkis teaching the people.

"The High Priest was angry and declared that the words of Jezreen were against the way of Zeldin and Imarko, but the Prince insisted that Zeldin himself had ordered him to teach new thoughts to Galkis.

"When the Twelfth Emperor died, the High Priest urged his successor to banish his brother but Jezreen entered the palace and challenged the new Emperor to a game of Zel. The Thirteenth Emperor was a famous player and proud of his skill, so he accepted the challenge and the high stakes. If the Emperor won, Jezreen would leave Galkis for ever. If Jezreen was victor, he might stay. They played for twelve hours and Jezreen spoke aloud his meditations between every move. The Emperor marvelled at the wisdom they revealed. He forgot to guard the invisible piece at the centre of the board and lost the game.

"From that day, Jezreen lived in a cave in the foothills of the mountains above Galkis. Many came up from the city to hear him teach, even the Emperor's three sons, and they wrote down their uncle's words.

"One day, when the Prince was very old, as he sat at a solitary game of Zel, a zeloka was seen to fly to the mouth of his cave. When Jezreen's followers saw the marvellous bird they knew that Zeldin had summoned their master. He took his staff and followed the zeloka up into the mountains. It was the last zeloka to be seen in Galkis and the last glimpse of Jezreen-lo-Kaash."

Forollkin tossed more wood on the fire. "You make me feel like a pupil again, all that sitting straight-backed on cold marble benches while priests intoned the Book of Chronicles."

"I would have loved to hear such stories every day," protested Gwerath.

"Not the same ones every day, surely, and besides, Kerish tells them better than a priest."

Forollkin smiled at his brother but Kerish said gravely, "There are still many who do not accept the teachings of Jezreen. Even Izeldon sometimes . . ."

"Oh, spare us the priestly wranglings." Forollkin yawned. "I'm sure Gwerath would rather hear about some of the Court Festivals."

He began to tell her about the roof-top processions during the Star-counting Festival.

Gidjabolgo played again for the Prince and whispered

above the music, "Your eyes are dark tonight. Does something displease you? Is it your brother's sudden change of heart? Or perhaps you have other sorrows. Are you affronted by the sight of happiness?"

"Are you?" asked Kerish sharply.

Gidjabolgo's face was in shadow as he bent over the zildar.

"Why yes. I will allow no-one happiness unless it diminishes my sorrows and not even then if it pleases another more."

"I won't think like that!"

At the misery in Kerish's voice even Gidjabolgo looked up.

"I won't." Kerish was already stumbling down the grassy slope. He ran across the pebbled beach and stood on the edge of the sea, struggling with the hatred that flowed through him.

Forollkin left Gwerath by the fire and strode down on to the beach. His heavy boots crunched on sand and pebbles. Kerish heard and turned to face his brother, thinking of a dozen greetings that would strike as sharply as a lash, and in the moonlight he saw the old scar on Forollkin's cheek. He looked into his brother's anxious grey eyes and the venemous words in his mind came out as a sob.

Then Forollkin was holding him tightly and saying ridiculously, "If you stand there in the water, you'll catch cold. Kerish, what's the matter?"

"Forollkin, whatever I might say, I don't want to mean it. Please believe me!"

"Kerish, I'm sorry, I don't understand, you'll have to tell me. Is it something about Gwerath? I know I've been stupid, but I'm doing my best now to put things right. Isn't that what you wanted? I promise to try and make her happy."

Too shocked to answer, Kerish stared at his brother's earnest face as Gwerath called down to them.

"Are we going back to the boat now? Shall I damp down the fire?"

Forollkin shouted back, "Yes," and gave his brother a shake. "Kerish, you're shivering. I knew you'd catch cold."

120

Two mornings later, Forollkin was the first to sight the cliffs of Silnarnin as they rounded a headland and sailed into the Straits of Chire. For the next few days Gidjabolgo tried to keep the *Starflower* to the calm water midway between Chiraz and the island. At dawn on the fourth day, in spite of all his skill, the boat was caught in a fierce current and swept towards the maze of rocks that surrounded the gaunt cliffs of Silnarnin.

Trying to keep some control, Gidjabolgo bellowed out orders. Forollkin and Gwerath hurried to obey, while Kerish hung over the rail watching the approaching rocks.

"That one looks almost like the parapet of a tower," he said dreamily, as Forollkin rushed past him to the prow.

"Kerish, help me a moment!" Gwerath was clinging doggedly to a rope that was burning the palms of her hands.

Kerish added the strength of his good hand to hers, but he shouted above the noise of the sea, "Don't worry. I think we should let the current take us. Shubeyash drew us to Tir-Roac, perhaps Vethnar is drawing us to Tir-Melidon."

"And do we know that he wants to see us?" Forollkin had overheard. "Or anything about him?"

"No," admitted Kerish.

For a moment everyone lost their balance as the current swerved towards a jagged line of rocks, pulling the *Starflower* with it.

Gidjabolgo swore at the tiller and Forollkin stepped forward to steady Gwerath. She leaned against him for a few seconds, her silver hair catching in the buckle of his cloak. Giddy and drenched they flinched as the rocks seemed to leap at their frail craft, but within moments the *Starflower* had been swept into a deep channel.

To either side the waters seethed, tormented by the rocks beneath, but for the moment their danger was forgotten in the excitement of a discovery.

"It is a tower!" insisted Kerish.

The others crowded round him to stare at the dark, shell-encrusted stone.

"Look, every time the water falls, it uncovers a window, with faces carved on the lintel."

"They're too grotesque for anything but the sea to have shaped them," protested Forollkin.

"And that must be the top of a stair." Kerish pointed with his good hand. "Watch how the foam pours through the balustrade."

Forollkin shaded his eyes against the spray. "If it's a staircase, where did it lead to?"

"Look at that rock!" Gwerath grabbed Forollkin's arm. "It's got writing on it."

"I can see a sort of pattern," said Forollkin grudgingly, "but it might be natural."

"If *that* was made by wind and wave, I fear this sea."

"Where, Gidjabolgo?"

They all turned to look where the Forgite was pointing and Forollkin was silenced.

A circle of rock formed a natural pool and above its dark waters rose a long head, tilted towards the sky. The crystal inlay of its three eyes glittered in the morning sun and the ridges that broke the surface on either side of the head might have been the tips of vast, furled wings.

The current swept them through the drowned buildings, past gables, pinnacles and battlements and each of the travellers imagined the city stretching down below them and the inhabitants that might tread its water streets.

At noon, Kerish fetched some food from the cabin and the others ate where they worked.

"Does there seem anything strange to you about those cliffs ahead?" asked Gidjabolgo as he snatched his favourite from a basket of fruit that the Prince held out to him.

They were fast approaching the easternmost point of Silnarnin but nothing could be seen of the island, no beaches, no grassy slopes, no trees against the skyline, only sheer walls of iron grey rock.

"On Hemcoth's charts, there's no harbour marked, no break in the cliffs at all," continued the Forgite, "yet somehow I can't quite believe their fierceness."

Kerish closed his eyes.

"They're real enough," he said after a moment, "but . . ."

In his mind's eye, faint lines appeared on the rock and the

lines darkened into arched windows with panes of crystal. A hand opened one of the casements and a figure leaned out to gaze at the sea far below him.

Kerish had a brief impression of a pale face and a shock of red hair. Then he knew that the figure had become aware of him. The window slammed shut. Kerish opened his eyes and the cliff-face was as blank as before.

"We're looking at Tir-Melidon," he said, "at Vethnar's citadel."

As he spoke, the *Starflower* shuddered, dipped to one side and lurched forward. Gidjabolgo sprang up and peered over the rail. The wind was slight and the sails hung slack but the *Starflower* was moving eastwards faster than before. Forollkin pounded along the deck towards them, followed by Gwerath, a half-eaten fruit forgotten in her hand.

"What's happening?"

"The current is quickening," growled Gidjabolgo.

Forollkin strained to hear above the immediate noise of waves on rock.

"It sounds like the rumble of a landslide. Kerish, you've got the best eyes, can you see anything?"

The boat was rocking violently and their speed whipped up a cloud of spray but after a few moments Kerish made out two pillars of black rock and beyond them the restless agony of a whirlpool.

"Rope yourself to the rail," he shouted, "there's a whirlpool ahead!"

Gwerath sprang to fasten the hatches while Forollkin got out the ropes to loop about their waists. He left himself till last and as his hands struggled to knot his rope securely, the boat plunged into a deep trough. Water poured across the deck, slamming Gwerath against the mast.

Gidjabolgo also lost his balance but he scrambled up from the slippery boards as the *Starflower* jutted towards the sky on the crest of a wave. He grabbed at Kerish, and Gwerath and Forollkin clung to the mast.

The timbers screamed in protest as the *Starflower* was dragged towards the whirlpool. The spray was blinding and the noise deafening. Greedily the white waters seized the boat again and it span in narrowing circles towards the sucking darkness.

Suddenly the prow was twisted round and the *Starflower* plunged northwards. Another wave struck the deck and only Gidjabolgo's painful grip kept Kerish upright, but his eyes were still open and he saw the cliff-face looming above them.

"Zeldin!" He waited for the impact and there was sudden darkness. "How quickly it's over," thought Kerish. "Death doesn't hurt at all."

Then Gidjabolgo's shaking fingers tugged at his hair.

"Ouch, let go."

Forollkin was calling to him. "Kerish, is that you? Are you all right."

"Yes, both of us. What's happening? We're still moving."

"We must have entered some kind of tunnel."

Each word echoed.

Unfastening the rope around his waist, Forollkin felt his way along the rail to the hatchway, and went below to get a light. After much fumbling in the pitch black cabin he managed to get two lamps alight.

Back on the deck he held the lamp high. Gwerath knelt beside the mast looking very small and young with her long hair sleeked with spray. Gidjabolgo was wringing the water from his cloak but Kerish stood motionless in his sodden robe, his left hand gleaming as if he still held the Jewel of Zeldin in his crippled fingers.

"You look like a half-drowned kitten, Gwerath," said Forollkin, remembering Lilahnee when Kerish had first found her in the marshes. "I've lit another lamp below. Go down and change your clothes."

"Let me see where we are first."

But though Forollkin swung the lantern round, its flame was too weak to pierce the outer darkness.

He called out and listened to the booming echoes. "The roof must be high. We're in a large cave rather than a tunnel."

They could no longer hear the noise of the sea, only the rushing of the subterranean waters that bore them northwards. Gwerath started towards the hatch, her boots squelching with each step, but suddenly darted to the rail.

124

"Look, look there!"

The others were quickly beside her, but saw nothing.

"It's gone," sighed Gwerath, "a silvery light, moving just below the water."

She had begun to shiver violently and Forollkin looked at her anxiously. "Hurry up and change."

Gwerath came back in a grey Seldian dress with a blanket draped round her shoulders and sat down on a coil of rope to rub the salt from her wet hair. When the others had changed into their spare clothes, Forollkin handed round cups of wine to help warm them.

"Well, Kerish, perhaps we *are* under this sorcerer's protection." Forollkin raised his cup in a vague salute. "Though when I saw that whirlpool, I thought our quest would end there."

"I thought for a moment it had," admitted Kerish. "I thought I was dead."

"So did I," murmured Gwerath.

"And was my Mistress pleased to find that death was not oblivion?" asked Gidjabolgo.

"I was angry," said Gwerath unexpectedly. "The Hunter promised us rest."

"Well I was just grateful." Forollkin poured himself more wine. "And, besides, your finger nails were digging into my arm all the time. There's nothing like pain to reassure you that you're alive."

The cup suddenly slipped from Gwerath's hand as she started up. "Look, there is the light again, but more gold than silver."

"That's too high to be in the water . . ." began Forollkin.

"It's daylight surely," broke in Gidjabolgo.

Kerish was the last to turn towards it. With each second the bright hole extended but it still seemed too small for the *Starflower* to pass through and Kerish sat with hunched shoulders while the others stood in the prow.

A fresh breeze rippled her sails and the *Starflower* glided out on to the crystalline waters that filled a huge crater, ripped by some great explosion from the centre of Silnarnin.

From the placid lake the ravaged hills rose up more gently

than the outer cliffs and their slopes were covered with tall grasses and shapely trees. In the rock-face, high above an arc of white sand, glittered the many windows of Vethnar's citadel, but at first the travellers noticed none of this. Their bodies vibrated to the deep, sweet cries that swept across the crater.

Kerish sat up straight and found himself looking into a prism, constantly splitting into new fragments. The colours flowed about and through him and the sense of loss he had felt in Tir-Roac flooded back. He bowed his head and the same colours shone unseen in his own tears.

The others saw that the air was full of shapes in ecstatic flight. Above the prow arched two golden creatures with wings like sheaves of sunlight and a third, its mane a cluster of crescent moons, stretched its opaline coils half-way across the lake. For a moment a living rainbow swirled about the *Starflower*'s mast and, beneath the dazzling colours, the lovely shape of its bones shone white and the veins flowed with crimson fire.

For as far as they could see, the creatures burnished the air but some of the shapes were nearly lost in frozen torrents of jewels, while others, further off, glowed with a darker light. Gwerath realized that Forollkin was gripping her shoulder.

"I think it's all right," she murmured. "Look how beautiful they are!"

Forollkin stared in wonder at the amber glory of a creature caught forever in the highest leap of some wild dance, but Kerish still sat with bowed head and the expression on Gidjabolgo's face was closer to fear than wonder.

A cerulean cloud spiralled with silver, moved towards them, its reflection lancing the waters with pure light. But as they watched, the silver ceased to undulate, stiffened by some unseen frost. Beautiful in despair, the blue form writhed and twisted to escape from its silver cage.

Then with a sudden crunching, the *Starflower* ran aground on the white sand and Kerish looked up again.

"We're below Tir-Melidon."

Beneath the lowest windows, splayed against the slope

was a creature, huge as a castle. Its petrified wings glimmered like a dragonfly's and its tangled mane ran like a river of gold towards the lake, hiding the great head.

"I can't see an entrance," said Forollkin. "We'll have to climb past the windows, up the slope, to the top."

He leapt ashore, as Gidjabolgo began to secure the boat. The others followed. Kerish went up to his ankles in the white sand as he jumped from the rail. He recovered without the help of Gwerath's proffered hand and joined Forollkin a little way down the beach.

The young Galkian was staring at another of the creatures. In shape it was like a cluster of half-opened flowers but its body was stained with a darkness like the smoke of incense. Parts of its skin were hard and bright as glass and Kerish glimpsed himself reflected in petals that enclosed a lidded eye. He thrust out a hand to hide the sight. His fingertips brushed a petal and it crumbled away, revealing a hollow blackness.

They all looked back towards the *Starflower* and saw a silver and blue shape hanging quite motionless on the air.

Forollkin's voice cracked as he spoke. "Let's get up that slope! There's a sort of path to the left here."

They left the sand and followed a track through the tall grasses, with Gidjabolgo hurrying to catch them up. Their way was often barred by the creature stretched across the slope. At first they stepped carefully over its glittering coils, but as the slope grew steeper, Gidjabolgo began using them as footholds as he helped Kerish to climb one-handed.

They paused to rest beside one unfurled wing and marvelled at the unknown colours gleaming through the limpid skin but, here and there, the wing was encrusted with dark jewels like the symptoms of some terrible sickness and Kerish was glad that the golden waterfall of hair hid the face.

Ten minutes' hard climbing brought them level with the lowest windows of Vethnar's citadel. Only one was accessible.

Normal courtesy long forgotten, Forollkin sidled along a narrow ledge, leapt, caught at the sill and raised himself for a few seconds to peer in.

"What did you see?" demanded Gwerath eagerly.

She had kilted up her grey dress and her hair was drying into a stiff mass of silver.

He smiled at her. "Little enough. Just a small room with a single chair in it facing a wall I couldn't see."

The last part of the slope was mantled with tiny white and golden flowers whose sweet scent attracted clouds of insects. Forced onto hands and knees it was an undignified climb for the travellers and not everyone escaped stings as they disturbed the insects. Forollkin scrambled up the last few yards and onto the summit, quickly followed by Gwerath and Gidjabolgo. As Kerish clambered onto flat ground and picked himself up, he heard the others exclaim. The whole sky was filled with a mass of rich blue and mottled green, crowned with great golden coils. It took him a few seconds to realize that he was looking at a gigantic flower.

"May a sorcerer never," began an irritated voice, "be granted solitude, even in his own citadel?"

Kerish felt for a moment that he was falling very fast and then he blinked as his eyes re-focused on a small blue flower, half-hidden in the grass.

Beside it stood the sorcerer of Tir-Melidon.

Chapter 8

The Book of the Emperors: *Chronicles*
Great was his learning and all praised him, save the Empress his mother. One day, as he read to her from his history of the First Battle of Viroc, she began to weep. He was amazed and questioned her saying: "Mother, why are you sad? Is it for the many who died in defence of their city?" And she answered him: "I weep because for you they have never lived. The dead are frail as figures cut from paper by your thoughts, like dolls for a beggar's child." The Emperor smiled at his mother's fancy but the Empress said: "My son, promise that you will never write of me. The patterns you make with your paper figures may please those who are afraid to weep but I will not be part of them."

THE travellers had all seen merchants from Kolmandis, dark-skinned, stately and silent, but Kerish had the sudden ridiculous conviction that Vethnar was only dressed up as a Kolgorn to play some elaborate trick.

The Lord of Tir-Melidon was as black as the screaming rocks of Cheransee, with tightly curled hair, the dull bronze of an ancient sword, but he was far from silent.

"The Mountains of Chire, a drowned city, whirlpools, cliffs . . . all are useless to protect me. I might as well study in the market place of Kolmandis; at least the street-urchins might be awed into silence and not trample on my visions!"

Vethnar was leaning on a staff of polished ebony. He seemed little older than Forollkin but, even stooping, he was a head taller. He wore a shapeless brown robe that fought a constant battle to encumber the violent gestures of his right arm.

"Now here is a whole afternoon's work lost!"

The lean dark fingers jabbed the air in the general direction of Forollkin, who began a startled apology.

129

The sorcerer cut him short. "It is to your children and your children's children that you should apologize!"

"Vethnar, you knew they were coming. You told me so yourself, not half an hour ago."

For the first time, the travellers noticed a plump old man sitting cross-legged on the turf a little way behind the sorcerer. A role of parchment was stretched across his lap and beside him were pots of ink and a jar of quill pens.

"What if I did, child?" snapped Vethnar. "During journeys of the mind it is most disturbing to be suddenly made to view the whole again."

"The drawings were almost complete," said the other firmly.

"Drawings of that flower?" asked Kerish.

"Of course." Vethnar squatted down beside the old man. "Show them, Dolodd."

The travellers looked over Dolodd's shoulder at a series of exquisite drawings of petals and stamens.

"Men never look at things," muttered Vethnar, "not *really* look, as I do, concentrating on a single blossom until it fills their whole world."

"Perhaps we don't have the time," said Dolodd, rolling up the parchment. "Fifty years would be a very long time for a mortal to spend looking at flowers."

"Hah! You mortals think fifty seconds is too long! You're obsessed with seeking outwards and spurn the treasures at your feet. Why can't you keep still and enrich yourself with what's in front of you instead of grabbing at impossibilities?"

"Surely it must be possible," said Kerish earnestly, "for the mind to enrich itself through the body's restlessness?"

"Well, I warn you it is not," declared Vethnar, "and I am the sorcerer of Tir-Melidon."

"And I am Kerish-lo-Taan." The Prince seized his chance. "And this is my brother Lord Forollkin."

"And him?" Vethnar pointed eagerly at Gidjabolgo.

"This is our companion, Gidjabolgo of Forgin."

"Good, you look a quarreller and that's what I need."

"And this," persisted Kerish, "is my cousin Gwerath, a Princess of the Sheyasa, from Erandachu."

"A woman?" Vethnar got up to peer suspiciously at Gwerath. "No, no use at all."

"I've told you before," said Dolodd as he began to gather up his inks. "If you really want all opinions you should welcome women."

"Why, does this one talk?"

"Like a cage full of Dik-birds," answered Gidjabolgo.

"I knew a woman once who talked," murmured Vethnar, "moon-silver hair she had, just like that. She did nothing but interrupt our studies. Saroc and I worked well together before she lured him to her and soured his life."

"You wrong Sendaaka!"

The Prince's reproof clashed with Gwerath's indignant, "Of course I can talk! I carry the lore of my tribe, and I . . ."

"Vethnar, you have offended all your guests." Dolodd hauled up his comfortable bulk. "You must make amends."

"Have I? How interesting. You must tell me how. But later, later, I know my duty."

The sorcerer slashed a mark in the turf with the tip of his ebony rod and a circle of grass dissolved away to reveal a flight of steps.

"Come down into my citadel."

It was Dolodd who showed the Galkians and Gidjabolgo to a set of rooms overlooking the sea, before escorting Gwerath to her quarters. The first room was plainly furnished with three couches and a low table but the one set aside for Kerish was elaborately decorated in the fashion of ancient Galkis. The bed was hung with Imperial purple, a tapestry depicting the Poet Emperor and the Trieldiss covered one wall, and a vase of ice blue cirge filled with orchids stood on a window-sill. Kerish's possessions had already been brought up from *Starflower* and arranged on a table. Since no chests had been provided for his clothes, these, neatly folded, were laid upon the bed.

Forollkin's room was decorated with exotic swords and axes and a vivid painting of scenes from the Battle of Viroc, while Gidjabolgo's was crammed with gaudy treasures to imitate the vulgar splendours of a Forgite mansion.

"If there is anything you dislike," said Dolodd, "Vethnar will change it for you. Don't be afraid to ask. The rooms have been prepared for weeks, of course. Let nine out of ten of his words slip past you. They mean nothing, but seize on the tenth and worry at it till you're sure you know its meaning."

Forollkin took down a scimitar that hung precariously over his pillow.

"That sounds no easy task to me."

"It isn't," agreed Dolodd. "I've had thirty years' practice and still mistake him once in a while. I will return for you later."

Forollkin sat down cautiously on the striped skin with dangling claws that sprawled across the bed and stared at the mural. He was forced to admit that the half-severed arm of the barbarian leader and the dying Galkian trampled beneath the hooves of his own horse were marvellously painted.

"I'll give you a silk sheet off my bed to hang over it," said Kerish, "in return for one of your blankets."

"Accepted, dearest brother, and I'm glad it's your task to talk to our host."

"I fancy this sorcerer will expect you to talk as much as anyone; he clearly has no taste for shyness."

"Then he should enjoy Gidjabolgo's company."

The Forgite was occupied in stacking some of the more atrocious ornaments under his bed. Then he and the others explored a narrow passage that led to a small chamber with a bath sunk in the rock crystal floor. Three ewers and basins of lapis stood beside it but all were empty and there was no visible means of filling them or, apparently, any servants to summon.

"No, there are no servants here," said Dolodd when he returned. "The power of Vethnar attends to all our needs, but I grant you he's often forgetful or thoughtless. There's a fountain behind the green door across the passage. You could fetch water from there, but there's no time now. Follow me and try to remember the way. It's not easy but the patterns that cover the floors are different on each level, which helps a little."

The companions followed Dolodd down a passageway patterned with jet flowers blossoming in a sea of amethyst.

Forollkin tried to place their guide, with his pale wrinkled skin, lively black eyes and thick grey hair elaborately dressed in tufts and coils.

"Where do you come from, Dolodd?"

"From Dard. I was sailing in my father's ship with a cargo of Dik feathers for Losh-Mindar when our sorcerer caught me."

"Caught?"

"The captain was a fool to sail so close to Silnarnin, but Vethnar is not greedy, he only took me. Now here's your Lady's rooms."

He knocked on a low door glowing with waves of amber crested with foamy pearls. As he opened it the corridor echoed with the sound of helpless laughter.

"Stay there, Kerish," ordered Forollkin after one glance, and he stepped inside.

Gwerath sat amongst the down pillows on a bed draped with shell-pink silk. Walls and ceiling were covered with mirrors and even the marble floor was polished to reflect her every movement. The room was half-filled by row upon row of chests, each overflowing with velvet robes, embroidered gowns, veils, dainty slippers, phials of perfume, hair-pins, bracelets and every conceivable jewel and trinket. The only other furnishings were twelve vases crowded artlessly with flowers that thickened the air with their cloying scents.

Gwerath had wound a rope of pearls twice round her slender neck and they still reached her knees. She giggled again at the myriad reflections of this absurdity.

"Oh Forollkin, I shall suffocate in here! What can I do?"

"We could put the vases in the corridor," began Forollkin doubtfully, "and perhaps I could push some of the chests back against the walls."

Gidjabolgo peered round the door and scowled at himself in the mirrors.

"By the Nostrils of Golmion! A chamber fit for a Loshite to languish in!"

"Gwerath, get up, the sorcerer is waiting!"

"Yes, Forollkin."

With untrustworthy meekness, the Princess of the Sheyasa

133

stripped off the pearls, smoothed her unruly hair and joined her companions.

They soon lost all sense of direction as Dolodd led them along winding passages and up and down spiral stairs till they came to a long chamber with windows overlooking the crater.

"Welcome again!" Vethnar jumped up from his place at an oval table and beckoned to Kerish and Gwerath to sit amongst the cushions heaped on either side of him.

Forollkin found Dolodd on his right and a thin, red-haired boy on his left. Gidjabolgo was seated opposite Vethnar, between a grizzled warrior in a snake-skin tunic and a younger man, whose flaxen hair and copper skin marked him as an Ellerinonn.

In front of each place was an alabaster cup of spring water, a dish of raw meat and vegetables and a pearl-handled fork. Cauldrons were set into the centre of the table. One was filled with oil that bubbled and spat, the others with hot pungent liquids.

"Now, before we eat," began Vethnar, "introductions. Prince Kerish, Lord Forollkin, Master Gidjabolgo and Princess . . ."

"Gwerath."

"Princess Gwerath. Now us. That frightful red hair belongs to Breldor and he's another Forgite, Gidjabolgo. On your right is Rezag-Khal, a worthy warrior of Chiraz, and beside you, Kerish, is Llartian, from Tir-Rinnon. Dolodd you already know. I'm sure you've had half his history already and the rest you won't escape for long."

A basket of bread was passed around the table and Dolodd showed the travellers how to impale strips of raw meat on their forks, cook them in the boiling oil and dip them in the sauces.

From one of his copious sleeves, Vethnar drew out a silver pot of some strongly scented spice which he proceeded to shake over everything he ate.

"Flevel. I was bred on it," he explained. "Have you ever tasted Orga meat? No? Well if you had you'd know why all Kolgorns smother their food with spices. I can't seem to break the custom; it's an interesting example of . . ."

"Before we start," interrupted Dolodd, "shouldn't you ask if your guests are happy with their quarters?"

"Yes, I should," said Vethnar amiably. "Are you?"

Kerish and Forollkin prepared to be polite but Gwerath said firmly, "No. I have never seen anything so ridiculous. Why should I want all those chests of clothes and jewels? There's no room to move and I don't want any mirrors."

"I assure you I took great pains to read about what women like." The sorcerer sounded genuinely taken aback. "And surely you can't object to the sight of your own beauty."

"I am not beautiful," said Gwerath quietly.

"Nonsense, you're very like her. What about you, Gidjabolgo?"

Like Gwerath, Gidjabolgo had no qualms about speaking his mind. "You have the taste of my people to perfection. Now all I need is a golden bowl to vomit in."

"Breldor," cried the sorcerer, "I did your rooms just the same to make you feel at home. You like them, don't you? You've never complained."

"Sir . . . I mean Vethnar, I'm very grateful," the boy plucked nervously at his red hair, "but I don't really care for . . ."

"Ah, I see now that both of you dislike your countrymen. How interesting. So do I." Vethnar impaled a sliver of meat on his fork. "Silent as Kolgorn, that's what men say. Stupid as Kolgorn, it should be."

"The Kolgorns I have met before," began Llartian, "have been dignified and serious men who . . ."

"Hah! Too dignified ever to admit natural ignorance. There is no sin as great in Kolgor as asking questions that your elders can't answer."

Kerish smiled. "I take it that you committed this sin."

"As often as I could, till I grew sick of them and they of me. Then I stole my uncle's best Orga and rode across the desert to Roac . . . don't flinch, it was a living land then and Shubeyash was still Crown Prince, but famous for his learning."

Vethnar plunged his fork into the oil and held it there, unnoticing, while the meat blackened.

135

"He received me with great kindness. For years we studied together but I saw how it might be and turned away from the path he trod. I asked leave to go to Gannoth and when Shubeyash saw that he could not dissuade me, he loaded me with gifts and sent me in his own ship. I haven't thanked you, have I, Kerish? Shubeyash was my dearest friend."

"His spirit is at rest now," said the Prince.

Vethnar nodded. "The shadow he cast was long. I am glad he has stepped into the light again. I might as well say at once that there is nothing I can do about your hand, Kerish, except seat you next to our thoughtful Llartian."

The Ellerinonn had been quietly breaking Kerish's bread into manageable pieces but now he looked directly at the sorcerer. "I was sent from Ellerinonn to help others, Vethnar; there are few enough ways that I can carry out my task trapped in your citadel."

Vethnar stared back into Llartian's candid, grey eyes.

"You under-estimate my ingenuity on behalf of my guests but surely you should rejoice if your fellows are too content to need help."

"I do not recall Rezag-Khal expressing his content."

The sullen warrior from Chiraz still did not speak for himself.

"Surely," exclaimed Vethnar, "you cannot disapprove of my saving him from death, when he was bound to his shield and cast into the sea? I grant that he is far from talkative and therefore of little use to me but if I send him back, the Khan of Chirandermar will kill him."

"My sentence was just." The old man moved his cropped head like an animal troubled by insects. "Just."

"So you have said before." There were shades of irritation in Vethnar's voice, "But not why. To punish yourself for a fault you could not help seems to me to be cowardice. Would you agree, Breldor?"

The boy gulped down a mouthful of food and said hesitantly, "Do you mean that everyone should recognize that failure is natural to our present state and learn to live bravely with that knowledge?"

"I might . . . but is it what you would say?"

136

"Yes, yes, I think it is."

Vethnar powdered the blackened meat on his fork with flevel.

"There, Dolodd, didn't I tell you what a fine catch this boy was? I'll be better pleased still when he learns how to disagree with me intelligently."

"But not better pleased should he actually *do* anything you disagree with," said Llartian sharply, "like leaving your citadel."

"Not everyone is as anxious as you are, Llartian, to be buffeted by the storm-winds of the world again but you need not fret. Elmandis will eventually find out where you are and then I shall have to give you back, for you know his temper . . . Forollkin, you've stopped eating. Perhaps you'd prefer to talk to us instead; a brief address on the true nature of heroism . . ."

Forollkin looked desperately at his brother and Kerish took pity on him.

"The Book of the Emperors states that bravery is often divided from boorishness only by the cloak of modesty. I believe that the Five Kingdoms hold a contrary view and think boasting a virtue. What do the men of Dard say, Dolodd?"

"Oh, never ask a Dardik about bravery," said Dolodd lightly. "It takes no courage to strip a Dik–bird of its feathers. We have no enemies, are too lazy to fight each other, and make no bones about saying so."

"I see no harm in a man saying he is strong or brave, if it is true," said Gwerath.

During the previous conversation she had been too busy eating and staring round the room to listen.

The walls of the chamber were faced with blue stone and its narrow windows were set too high to see out of from where they sat. The table and cushions were the only furnishings but in a niche, a large book lay open. Gwerath watched it with fascination, since every few minutes its pages would turn, though no-one stood near it. She heard the rustle of vellum as Kerish answered.

"No harm, if he remembers that strength and courage are not good in themselves. It is the ends for which they are used that matter."

"That is very true, Prince," said Llartian gravely. "I imagine it takes courage to murder in cold blood."

"You speak of good and bad ends." Gidjabolgo's cup seemed shocked into pallor by the coarseness of the hand that gripped it. "Would you say we have the freedom to mistreat ourselves?"

"Yes." Llartian's affirmative clashed with Kerish's denial and Breldor's hesitant, "No, I think not."

"If you say no," pursued Gidjabolgo, "you must condemn the heroism that causes men to risk death in a trivial cause of honour. Is that not an insult to the gift of life?"

"Ah, I see your argument." Vethnar leaned across the table. "You claim that a man's first duty is to preserve himself. Who will answer that?"

"Perhaps," said Kerish slowly, "if a man risks his life for someone else, that life is enriched, even in the losing of it. That would be no insult."

Llartian nodded his flaxen head. "The more you give, the more room you have to receive."

"Then the more you do for others, the more you profit yourself? A neat transaction!" exclaimed Gidjabolgo. "It seems we cannot lose."

Forollkin sat back among the cushions, watching his companions. Kerish seemed relaxed and confident, a half-smile on his lips as he waited to pounce on the Forgite's words. Gwerath was frowning slightly as she listened intently to Gidjabolgo, whose pale eyes sparkled with malicious pleasure. Vethnar's fingers sketched patterns of disagreement as Llartian carried on the argument, aided by Breldor's shy comments.

Forollkin understood everything that was said but nothing in him responded with new thoughts. He felt an outsider. Then Gwerath caught his eye and smiled at him. "I see no harm in a man saying he is brave or strong if it is true." Had she been thinking of him when she said that? Comfortingly, Forollkin decided that she had.

"Ah, Llartian," Vethnar was declaring, "you speak as your king has taught you. I remember Elmandis declaring once that he knew of higher powers but that he had no proof of a higher good and so worshipped nothing."

"I have my own opinions," insisted the Ellerinonn. "Our good king does not fetter our tongues."

"No, only your minds, and so lightly that you don't notice. Oh, you may protest," Vethnar went on quickly, "but I never knew a man so adamant as Elmandis upon having his own way in everything. He won Ellerinonn by conquest and, by conquest of his people's minds, he keeps it. Kerish, you have met this sorcerer king. Wouldn't you agree that he is convinced of the rightness of everything he does?"

"Yes, but of all the sorcerers we have met he seems the only one not to have wasted his powers, the only one to have tried consistently to use them for what he considers the good."

"All the sorcerers?" Vethnar smiled. "I beg you to reserve your judgement, Kerish. Tomorrow I will show you my library and you shall see what we do here and how I have occupied myself outside the tyranny of time."

Late that night, Dolodd's help was needed to find the way back to the travellers' apartments. With a sigh Gwerath opened the amber door and found her room quite changed. The mirrors had been replaced by plain walls, the flowers were gone and only one chest remained. Beside the bed, sombrely draped in grey, were two tables. One was piled high with books and neatly arranged on the other were a silver hand mirror patterned with stars, two ebony combs and a single windflower in a crystal vase.

Gwerath kicked off her shoes and sat down on the bed, staring around her in bewilderment. "How can everything have changed so quickly?"

Kerish closed his eyes for a moment.

"Very little of what Vethnar shows us is real." His hand stretched out to touch the back of the silver mirror. "Yet this is, and the combs."

In spite of Gwerath's yawns, Kerish stood looking down at them until Gidjabolgo said, "Can you tear yourself away, my Master? Or are we to help the lady to bed?"

With an apologetic smile Kerish hurriedly said goodnight.

At about two in the morning, Forollkin was woken by a
gentle but persistent tugging.

"Who . . . what's the matter?" He felt instinctively for
his sword.

"It's me," whispered Kerish, sitting down on the end of
the bed. "No, don't go back to sleep."

He prodded Forollkin, who had burrowed under his
pillows.

"Do you remember Vethnar saying that Shubeyash sent
him to Gannoth?"

Kerish took silence for assent.

"Sendaaka was Princess of Gannoth then. Do you think
he met her before Saroc?"

"Do I what?" Forollkin propped himself up on one
elbow, almost fully awake. "Kerish, it's the middle of the
night. What in Zeldin's name does it matter?"

"If a guess of mine is right, it may matter very much.
Forollkin, I, of all people, should know how much it hurts
and yet I'd use it against him if it would gain the key. What
kind of person am I?"

There was no mistaking the distress in his brother's voice
but Forollkin wondered sleepily if somehow he'd missed
half the conversation.

"Kerish, I don't know what you're talking about. Tell
me again."

As his eyes grew accustomed to the dim light, Forollkin
saw the Prince sitting with his crippled hand in his lap.

"There's more silver in your hair than there used to be."

It was Kerish's turn to look surprised.

"It must be curious," Forollkin went on, "never to be
allowed to look at yourself. I hadn't really thought about it
before."

"Oh, that's just the point. I do look at myself and I hate
what I see. Do you remember accusing me of doing more
than persuade people? Well, it's true. Sometimes I see into
them and I use what I see for my own ends. Surely that must
be evil."

"Kerish, you're having a nightmare. No-one could call you evil . . ."

"Stop laughing, Forollkin. In Galkis I was always making you do the things I wanted . . ."

"You were a horrible child," said Forollkin affectionately.

"But later, the terrible things I did to you . . . How could you forgive me?"

Forollkin grabbed at Kerish's wrist.

"Stop it! We won't ever talk about that. Do you hear, calm down!"

There was a moment's silence and then Kerish said softly, "I'm sorry to have woken you. I'll go back to bed now," and he slipped out of Forollkin's grasp.

Next morning, Gidjabolgo woke first and, after some exploration of the surrounding passages, came back lugging two ewers of water. Kerish had only just emerged from his room looking as if he had hardly slept, when there was a timid knock on the door and Breldor entered.

"I've come to take you to breakfast," he said. "We usually eat together in Dolodd's rooms."

Forollkin smiled at the boy. "Well, that's a welcome errand. Are there only the five of you living in this great citadel?"

"Yes. That is, I've never seen anyone else, but I haven't lived here long."

Forollkin finished buckling his cloak. "And have you explored the whole island yet, or is that forbidden?"

"No. We can go where we like," Breldor answered, "but there are only hills and woodland and . . ."

"The creatures of the lake," finished Kerish.

"Don't mention them in front of Vethnar," begged Breldor, "and don't look at them, if you can help it."

"Why?" demanded Gidjabolgo.

"If you watch them, you kill them."

The boy looked so miserable that Forollkin hastily said, "All right, we won't. Now lead us to breakfast. I, for one, am ravenous."

Gwerath emerged from her room, still wearing her grey dress and Forollkin's scarf knotted at her throat. Breldor led them down a spiral stair and they heard the roar of the sea through the slits in the rock that lit the way.

"It was you I saw leaning out of the window, wasn't it?" said Kerish.

Breldor coloured slightly. "Yes. Vethnar warned us not to but one of my windows overlooks the sea and I like to sit there for a while every day."

"Does it remind you of your home?" asked Kerish gently.

"Oh, no; except of the ruined watch-tower I found along the coast. I could hide my books there but my father found them."

"What happened then?"

"He burned them all. He burned them." Breldor spoke as if he could still hardly believe it. "And so I ran away."

"Do you like living with Vethnar?"

"Yes, more than anything I ever imagined. He is so clever and kind."

"If a trifle thoughtless," suggested Forollkin.

"No," the boy answered firmly, 'he remembers everything that is important."

Dolodd's apartments seemed to cover a whole floor of the citadel and were more sumptuously furnished than any they had yet seen. A table spread with gold and silver vessels stretched the length of a lofty banqueting hall and at the end of a row of forty chairs sat Llartian and the warrior of Chiraz.

"Dolodd has gone to the library to start work," said the Ellerinionn. "I am to take you there when we've breakfasted."

The previous night, Llartian had eaten nothing but bread but now his plate was piled high with fruit and Kerish remembered Soreas and his family and the meal he had enjoyed in their tranquil garden.

When they were all seated, Llartian lifted the lid of a silver jug and a rich aroma of fruit and spices filled the hall.

"Peshlinn; it's a Kolgorn drink. Usually there's milk or wine as well, but not this morning. So you'll have to try some."

He poured the steaming liquid into Gwerath's cup, then served the others.

"It's as delicious as the fruit of Ellerinonn," said Kerish after one sip.

"Nothing could be," answered Llartian, but he smiled.

"Rezag-Khal?" He offered the jug but the warrior shook his head, and sat stroking the pommel of his sword, staring at Gwerath, while the fruit was handed round.

Cautiously, Gidjabolgo slid the cover from a golden dish and revealed a heap of spice biscuits, elaborately shaped like fish or shells.

"I think they're meant to go with this," suggested Llartian, pushing a pot of something mauve and fluffy across the table, "but I'm not sure. Vethnar is fond of surprises."

"When I woke up this morning I found another present under my pillow," said Breldor. "Listen."

From a pocket in his grubby tunic he brought out a slender feather. The barbs were deep green patterned with crimson and gold and it cast a speckled light upon the table. He stroked the feather towards its tip and the chamber rang with bird-song.

"There was a note to say I mustn't stroke it the other way."

"And being you, I don't suppose you'll try." Llartian grinned. "I would, though."

Rezag-Khal suddenly writhed in his chair and with a stifled groan snatched at the silver jug. Though he had refused all food, now he filled his cup and drained it in one gulp. The veins bulged on his hands as he seized pieces of fruit and crammed them in his mouth till the juice streamed down his chin but all the while his eyes moved frantically as if beseeching help.

"Don't watch," said Llartian gravely. "He tried to starve himself to death. Now Vethnar forces him to eat."

"I should be at my work." Breldor replaced the shining feather in his pocket and scurried from the hall.

"Llartian," asked Forollkin abruptly, "why does Vethnar keep you here?"

"To talk to. If you go back to the chamber where we ate last night you will see a book in a niche and, if you look at the last few pages, you will find yourselves reading our recent conversation. There are hundreds of such volumes in Vethnar's library filled with the ideas and opinions of his guests over the centuries. You could spend a lifetime tracing patterns of thought amongst them and the curious thing is how often men of different lands and ages agree. Ah, I should warn you that any conversation Vethnar deems interesting enters his book, wherever it takes place and whether he was there or not. More peshlinn?"

The travellers all refused.

"Then I'll take you to the library."

As they rose to go Rezag-Khal, released from his compulsion, swept a hand across the table. Cups, bowls, and platters spun across the polished floor and a stream of peshlinn stained the snowy cloth. As if he had not noticed, Llartian asked the Chirazian to come with them and the old man nodded. Gwerath was afraid of the way his eyes still moved as if they were trapped. She imagined them bursting free and rolling like the plates across the floor towards her.

"Gwerath, is something the matter?"

She smiled hastily at Forollkin. "Nothing, just daydreams."

"Daydreams? In that dress you look as if you belong to twilight and stars, not day."

"You forgot to mention, Llartian, that peshlinn was intoxicating," remarked Gidjabolgo, "and some of us have weaker heads than others."

The Ellerinonn began an innocent protest.

"Oh, take no notice," said Gwerath crossly, "everything disagrees with Gidjabolgo."

Llartian led the travellers up a broad flight of steps to a noble archway, with Rezag-Khal trailing behind them, his snake-skin boots rasping against the marble.

"This is the entrance to the library. It fills more than half the citadel and I've not explored the whole yet."

"How long have you been here?" asked Forollkin.

"About seven months," answered Llartian. "I was sent from Ellerinonn to Losh-Mindar to help those who spend all and more than they have on the supposed pleasures of that city, but Vethnar caught me on the way."

They passed through a lofty hall, where clerestory windows lit shelf upon shelf of books bound in every shade of green. As they entered a second hall, filled with dark chests of scrolls and tablets of wood and clay, Kerish asked Llartian if he knew Soreas, his host in Tir-Rinnon.

"Only slightly, but I was in the city when you visited our King and I heard you singing about the Poet Emperor and his heart's desire."

A spiral stair of translucent stone, like the inside of some delicate shell, led them to an upper chamber, where the books were bound in blue and silver. Through an archway was a larger room, its trestle tables piled high with scrolls, some half-opened, others neatly tied with different ribbons.

Dolodd was bent over a desk beside the window, a quill in his hand.

"Vethnar, I tell you the Scroll of Tarnion must be on that table. I put it there myself."

"And I tell you it isn't. Oh, perhaps it is."

From the bottom of the pile the sorcerer detached a brittle scroll, bright with paintings of exquisite butterflies. Then he saw the travellers and dropped it again, provoking a wrathful snort from Dolodd.

"Ah, I'm glad you liked the peshlinn. Come and look at these."

He stretched out and weighted open several scrolls for their inspection, his dark face glowing with an enthusiasm that reminded Kerish of Hemcoth in his library.

Beside the butterflies were brief poems written in the curious script of Dard.

"There are eleven varieties of butterfly in the Dardic islands," Vethnar informed them. "It is said that an early Lord of Dard had eleven beautiful wives. Then he married a Princess of Gannoth who was jealous of the other wives and used her sorcery to turn them, one by one, into butterflies. The Lord was most displeased but he feared the Princess and did no more than make a garden where his former wives could live amongst the flowers and cluster about him . . . the garden is still there, is it not, Dolodd?"

"There is an ancient garden by the manor."

"And it is still forbidden in Dard to kill a butterfly. The

145

small one there is a Shereelia; she was supposed to be the prettiest wife."

"How lovely the blue sheen on its wings is," said Gwerath, "but Kerish paints as well as this. I remember the border of flowers and insects you once showed me . . ."

The Prince demurred but Vethnar looked very pleased.

"Excellent, royal blood and such accomplishments rarely go together. Hemcoth is another exception, of course. You cannot imagine how I have been tempted to steal him. He would be so much happier here. I cannot, as Gannoth is under my care and, though you disapprove of me, Llartian, I do have some sense of responsibility. Still, he would be a great help with the catalogue," finished Vethnar wistfully.

"You need an army, not just one stolen Prince, to finish this catalogue," put in Dolodd.

"Do you collect all kinds of books?" asked the Princess.

"I desire all knowledge." Vethnar still seemed a little uneasy when directly addressed by Gwerath. "So you will find all manner of books, history, poetry, legends . . . in every tongue of Zindar in my library and I, myself, have added a little over the centuries to this store of knowledge. At present we are looking at late spring, its flowers, birds, insects."

"Is that why it seems to be spring here when it should be autumn?" demanded Forollkin.

"Yes. I have kept it so for about two hundred of your years."

"Why does it take so long?"

"Why? A single patch of ground may contain a dozen different grasses and as many flowers and insects to be drawn and studied; enough to occupy me for fifty years. As I've said before, you humans are too shallow. You have no interest in details."

"I still don't really see why it matters," said Forollkin stubbornly.

Vethnar tugged ferociously at his sleeve and straightened to his full height. "If you wanted to make a cart or a boat and had no experience, what would you do?"

"Well, I suppose I'd . . ."

"You'd take one to pieces and see how it fitted together,

or at least look very closely, then copy it and perhaps improve on your model. Well, it's the same with Zindar. Men will never master their world till they've looked at every part of it, every part. Nothing could be more important. So you must understand, there can be no question of giving up my key. I've too much still to do. Now what would you like to see first?"

Kerish squeezed Forollkin's arm warningly and said, "Do you have any early copies of the Emperor Tor-Koldin's *Poems to the Moon's Gift*?"

"I have the original," declared Vethnar proudly. "In his own hand, if I can find it."

"Galkian room," said Dolodd without looking up from the labels he was inscribing. "The alcove nearest the window."

"Will you come with us?" asked the sorcerer humbly.

"No, too busy, but look out for Breldor on your way. I sent him down to Chronicles half an hour ago to fetch a scroll. He's probably lost."

"Only in a book, I'm sure," said Llartian.

After descending the shell-like stair they turned in a new direction and walked through a series of narrow galleries to a circular chamber where the books were bound in crimson leather.

Vethnar plucked one from a shelf. "This should interest you, Rezag-Khal – *The Lay of Chirandermar*, full of the high deeds of one of your Khans. Oh, I know you can't read but I'll teach you."

The Chirazian spat on the polished floor. "Reading is work for women and the maimed."

"Nonsense, we'll begin your lessons tomorrow." He turned to replace the book.

Swifter than a snake Rezag-Khal drew his dagger and plunged it in the sorcerer's back.

Too late, Forollkin seized his arm but Vethnar blew some dust from the crimson leather and said mildly, "You may hack at me all you will, if it makes you feel better, but I fear I cannot oblige you with any blood."

Stunned, Forollkin released the Chirazian. Rezag-Khal tore out his dagger and, growling with fury, tried to turn it on himself, but though sweat poured down his brow he could not move the weapon an inch towards his heart.

"It is useless. Listen to me." Vethnar gripped the warrior's shoulders and shouted at him as if to a deaf man. "You are going to live. Do you understand? Live, live, live!"

"The child of my Khan died," said Rezag-Khal. "He was in my keeping."

"It was an accident. Live to serve your Khan again if you cannot think of a better reason. Oh, take him away, Llartian. Take him and talk to him."

The Ellerinionn nodded and Rezag-Khal followed him, meek as the child he mourned so fiercely.

Vethnar led the travellers to a star-shaped chamber, lit by a single window. Nine chests contained rare scrolls and books bound in purple filled twelve alcoves about the walls.

"Ah here it is." Vethnar pounced on a slender volume whose ivory pages were filled with drawings of the Poet Emperor's cats and poems written in his own distinctive script.

"I had always heard," began Kerish "that this book was lost in the fire which destroyed the library at the Winter Palace of Joze."

"Lost books have a way of straying into my hands," replied Vethnar without embarrassment.

Gwerath exclaimed in delight at a sketch of the first Lilahnee curled up asleep on a rich robe of green brocade.

"That is the Robe of the Spring Festival," explained Kerish, "but when the Emperor found Lilahnee sleeping on the morning of the ceremony, he could not bear to wake her and went as he was, dressed in blue, so now the Robe of Spring is always blue."

The Prince read aloud several of the poems, translating into Zindaric, as Gwerath turned the pages, but his glance kept straying back to another volume upon the shelf: one bound in dark silk patterned with golden eyes. *The Book of Secrets.*

Vethnar was anxious to show the travellers more of his library so they soon left the Galkian room and were led through a bewildering maze of chambers and galleries, haunted by the smell of parchment and old leather. Often the sorcerer would pause and take down some favourite volume to display.

"Look at this, Gwerath, an account by an ancient Merchant of Forgin of a visit to Erandachu. He wrote down many legends and is most interesting on your religious customs, for example, the worship of . . ."

"Why is this door locked?" asked Kerish hastily.

"Oh, that's the Loshite room," said Vethnar, ever willing to be diverted. "Dolodd insisted I lock it up when Breldor arrived but I cannot, myself, see why. A few surprises never harmed anyone and besides, most of it seems very improbable. Ask for the key whenever you like. Now, I'm sure you'd be interested in the Seldian *Book of Queens* . . ."

They finally came to the Hall of Chronicles and found Breldor curled up on a window-sill, a heavy, iron-studded tome open across his knees. Through the crystal panes Kerish glimpsed a glorious flash of colour.

"Library windows are for letting in the light, not for staring out of," snapped Vethnar.

The boy jumped down apologizing.

"No matter, child. What were you reading?"

"*The Annals of the Khans of Zoanaxa.*"

"The account of the Battle of Serpent's Mound perhaps? A fine example of useless courage. You must read it, Forollkin."

But the young Galkian had been patient long enough.

"Sir, you refuse to give up your key. Well I'm sure my brother will have more to say to you concerning that but I should like things clear. Are we free to leave your citadel whenever we choose, or are we your prisoners?"

Vethnar closed the book carefully.

"You are my guests and very welcome, too."

"Yes, but . . ."

"See how upset you're becoming," said Vethnar solicitously. "You need rest after your arduous journey from Roac. In a few months, in the world's spring, you may go if you wish. In the meantime, wander where you will on Silnarnin."

When questioned the next morning, Kerish seemed to have no definite plan and merely urged his brother to enjoy his enforced rest. Exasperated, Forollkin could do nothing but follow that advice and so after breakfast he asked Gwerath to explore the island with him. Breldor was deputed to show them a stair to the surface while Gidjabolgo and Kerish returned to the library, where they found Dolodd.

The Forgite had borrowed Kerish's zildar and was soon ensconced amongst rare scrolls of music from all over Zindar, teaching himself new songs. The Prince stayed longer with Dolodd, learning, with all his customary quickness, something of the workings of the great library.

As Kerish leant over his desk the old man studied him — the pure, impassive profile, the dark downcast lashes hiding eyes of startling brilliance.

"It would be better for you to stay, you know. I don't understand exactly what you want of Vethnar, but it's clear that he won't give it. You can't go forward and there's never any purpose in going back. If you're anything like Breldor, and I fancy you are, you can't have been happy at the court of Galkis but here you could be. I'd be easier in my mind if I knew that he and Vethnar would have you for company when I'm gone."

"Gone? Surely this citadel lies outside time . . ."

"So it does," agreed Dolodd, "but a man's length of years and a peaceful death is all I ask."

"And will Vethnar permit it?"

"He's tried for over thirty years to argue me out of it, but storm and bluster as he may, he'll not deny my right to die."

"Yet he has no respect for Rezag-Khal's right to die."

"Oh, he would have, if the man produced a good enough argument. Why don't you stay? Breldor will never stand up to Vethnar but you could deal with his quirks and fancies. He needs a firm hand."

"And affection?" asked Kerish.

"And love," answered Dolodd. "That poem you asked about on the building of the Western Wall . . . you'll find it

150

in *The Snow-Book of Keshilarn*. Galkian room; just to the right of the door."

For an hour Kerish browsed amongst rare volumes brought from the nine great cities of Galkis and tried to ignore the one book he really wanted to read. No copies of *The Book of Secrets* ought to have existed outside the Imperial Palace and the Temple of Zeldin at Hildimarn. Kerish wondered how Vethnar had come by it and his fingertips brushed against the purple spine. In those pages there would surely be far more about the Saviour and his prison than could be gleaned from the poems and prophecies in the rest of *The Book of the Emperors*. If he could learn where the Saviour was imprisoned and by whom, then his quest would have a greater chance of success. It was his duty to read the book, in spite of it being forbidden . . . With unwelcome clarity, Kerish saw that Shubeyash must have reasoned in the same way when he searched for the forbidden knowledge that Roac had paid for so dearly.

"But I have no kingdom. I am the only one to pay for my mistakes . . ."

He took down the book and it seemed unnaturally heavy in his hands. Opened at random, the pages were a confused mass of colour. Then he realized that he was looking at a map, a map of the Imperial Gardens of the Inner Palace. It was obviously a very ancient map. Kerish recognized a few groves and pools and the Crystal Pavilion was marked but ruined shapes were painted all around it, as if the gardens concealed the remains of some vast building. He held the book closer, trying to decipher the single crabbed line of High Galkian that ran along the bottom of the map. "All that grows here is rooted in ancient sorrow."

"Dolodd told me you were here," said Vethnar from the doorway. "Did I make you jump?" He strode across the room and sat down beside Kerish, frowning at the blank vellum.

"Oh, *The Book of Secrets*. I went to a great deal of trouble to have that stolen from Hildimarn, only to find every page empty, but perhaps your eyes see more than mine. The eyes of the Godborn, how strange they are . . ."

He leaned forward and stared into the Prince's eyes as if

he was studying a rare flower or an interesting insect. Kerish flinched back and closed the book.

"Now, why did I come?" demanded Vethnar. "Ah, yes."

He delved into his sleeves and, with much jangling, finally brought out a bunch of keys.

"I know this is only a small consolation for the one I must refuse to give you but here are the keys to my citadel so that all my books are accessible."

"I can go wherever I like?"

"They open every door," promised Vethnar. "There are very few mysteries in Tir-Melidon. Tell your friends that."

"Thank you." Kerish replaced *The Book of Secrets* on its shelf. "Gidjabolgo will profit from your kindness, but my brother and my cousin have little time for scholarship."

"I thought your cousin seemed very interested in the scrolls I showed her."

"Gwerath loves all beautiful things and she knows truth when she sees it. There is very little that I can teach her."

For several minutes Kerish talked about Gwerath, praising her honesty and her intelligence. Vethnar sat drawing patterns in the dust on the window-sill, listening intently.

"Women are rarely wise," murmured the sorcerer, "but I have known exceptions."

"I have proof of her intelligence," said Kerish bitterly. "She sees through my pretensions."

"Why didn't you go with them to explore Silnarnin?"

"They don't need my company."

"He is helping her across a stream . . ." Vethnar seemed to be gazing through the rock walls of his citadel. "It is true that she looks happy but . . ."

"May I have the keys now?" Kerish asked abruptly.

"Of course."

Kerish took the heavy bunch of keys and left but Vethnar sat motionless for a long time.

"Silver hair," he said at last, "silver as stars in twilight."

For several days, Kerish explored Tir-Melidon and found, as Vethnar had promised, few mysteries. He unlocked every door and even went into the Loshite Room. Kerish glanced at one book, with fascinated disgust, and then hastily put it back on the shelf. On the second morning of his exploration he noticed a narrow stair in a corner of the Kolgorn Room. Above was an octagonal chamber full of books bound in plain black. Kerish opened one small volume. Its mouldering leather binding stank like a stagnant pond but the blood-red lettering of the incantations had not faded and on the first page were the words "*To Vethnar, my companion in learning, from Shubeyash, Prince of Roac.*"

On the third day, Kerish wandered through the lowest level of the library. At the end of a passage, flanked with baskets of clay tablets from Fangmere, was a low door. One-handed, Kerish clumsily tried a dozen keys in the silver lock and pushed open the door with his foot as the last one fitted.

He found himself in a room which he recognized at once from Forollkin's terse description. He sat down in the single chair that faced the north wall, where he could just make out the shape of a picture-frame hidden beneath a curtain of blue silk. There was nothing else in the room but a lingering scent of spice. For a long while he stared at the curtain. Then, without lifting it, he left the room and locked the door behind him.

On the same bright morning, Forollkin and Gwerath were exploring the wooded slopes of the western part of the island. By unspoken agreement they kept away from the crater and its creatures, staying within the sound of the sea. The cliffs were stark and silent but the island itself was full of birds singing from their nests in the trees or amongst the reeds that fringed the numerous pools and streams. The birds were very tame and would willingly perch on Gwerath's hand but the herds of goats were more timid. They had long soft coats of blue-grey, barred with brown and silver, and Gwerath would have liked to stroke one but they always scattered with bleats of panic as the travellers approached.

They reminded her of the wild Irollga of the plains and she began to talk about the painful process of learning to ride.

"I fell off once and bruised myself so badly that I refused to mount again. My father was so angry with me that I had to try and ride another Irollga and that time I didn't fall. The next day Father gave me a bridle with bronze studs. He had paid a trader four Irollga skins for it. I was so proud of that bridle."

They reached a brook. She sat down on a mossy stone, lifted her grey skirts and dipped her bare feet in the water.

"The windflower in the vase by my bed is still blooming, so it can't be real. They always die within a day of being picked."

Forollkin found himself a tree-stump and sat down, stretching out his long legs and tossing back hair, bleached by the long summer to a dusty gold.

"Starflowers are the same."

"What do starflowers look like?" asked Gwerath listlessly.

"They're purple, with a sort of golden centre," said Forollkin vaguely, "and their scent is very strong. I used to hate it as a child. When my mother found out, she stole some of the temple incense they make from the petals and had my nurse burn it in a brazier by my bed every night. I had to get accustomed to it because of the initiation ceremony. I told you about that didn't I?"

Gwerath nodded.

"The Emperor; did he love your mother?"

"He loved Kerish's mother."

"But surely he was fond of your mother?"

"Not particularly," answered Forollkin. "Nor of me."

Gwerath parted a clump of water-weed with her foot and startled a shoal of tiny speckled fish.

"It was the same for me. Tayeb always wanted a son."

"Well he nearly got one. You've a warrior's courage. Gwerath, what have I said . . .? Don't look so angry."

"I'm not. I know you think that women should be meek and dainty and drift about in silk and pearls like the fine ladies of Seld and Galkis. Well," she finished defiantly, "I could be like them if I wanted to, but I don't."

Forollkin tried vainly to imagine Gwerath at the Galkian court and what his mother would say about her.

"You could never be one of them."

"I thought you liked me to try," said Gwerath in a small voice. "I thought you wanted me to put up my hair and wear dresses."

"Not if it doesn't feel right to you."

He leaned over and gave an affectionate tug to the nearest silver braid.

"Gwerath, give me a little credit for liking you as you are. I don't want to change you, except perhaps to make you smile more often."

"Truly?"

"Truly."

His fingers tightened round her silver hair just as a voice came floating down to them.

"Hello, Forollkin, Gwerath. Come and give me a hand!"

The sorcerer of Tir-Melidon stood on the brow of a hill, waving and shouting.

"Come on, hurry!"

Forollkin shrugged resignedly.

"I suppose we had better see what he wants."

Gwerath nodded and kicked up a cloud of mud to dull the clear brook.

On the other side of the hill they found Vethnar bending over one of the goats who lay panting in a hollow, obviously about to give birth.

"She's having a hard time of it," announced the sorcerer, "but whenever I try to help her she butts me away. I need someone to hold her."

Forollkin found that he had stepped back a pace.

"Couldn't you ease her with a spell?"

"Well, I could," agreed Vethnar, "but that way I wouldn't learn anything."

The goat bleated her distress and her sides heaved as she struggled to get up. Gwerath knelt, pinioning the forefeet with her knees and gripping the horned head. Vethnar rolled up his sleeves.

"I hope you're enjoying your stay . . . there, there, easy now."

He stroked the heaving flanks and two small feet appeared.

"Wrong way round. I thought so. You know Forollkin, I really cannot imagine an excuse for being bored. Life is so interesting."

Forollkin closed his eyes as Vethnar took hold of the protruding legs.

A few minutes later, wet and gleaming, the kid slithered onto the grass. Vethnar brushed the birth-sac from its nostrils and it sneezed and began to wriggle.

"Can I borrow your dagger?"

Gingerly, Forollkin handed it over. Vethnar cut and knotted the umbilical cord.

"You can let her go now Gwerath."

The Princess released the horned head and the goat stumbled to her feet, nuzzled her kid and began to lick it vigorously. Vethnar wiped his bloody hands on his sleeves.

"I'm sorry to have disturbed your walk," he said cheerfully. "Now it's time to eat. Shall we go back together?"

At breakfast the next morning Gidjabolgo was absent and Kerish seemed so depressed and ate so little that Forollkin urged him to come exploring with them.

"There's a wood that reminds me of the Grove of Irnaald. Why don't you come with us and tell Gwerath the story of Irnaald and the Lady of the Rainbow?"

Kerish shook his head.

"Thank you, but I have some reading to do."

He drifted through the library towards the Galkian Room and *The Book of Secrets*.

Passing the Loshite Room he saw that the door was ajar and realized that he must have forgotten to lock it behind him. He felt for Vethnar's keys but a faint rustling betrayed that the room was not empty. Inside, Gidjabolgo sat hunched over a pile of gaudily bound books. He looked up as Kerish came in, waiting for contempt or disgust to appear on the Prince's face.

"Forgive me," said Kerish, unexpectedly, "I'd forgotten your quest. Have you asked Vethnar yet? Of all the sorcerers we've met he seems the most likely to . . . Gidjabolgo!"

He stared intently at the Forgite.

156

"You'd forgotten too, hadn't you?"

Gidjabolgo closed the book in his lap.

"I merely have less faith in Vethnar's generosity. Where is my other Master?"

"Walking somewhere, with Gwerath."

"My brains must be softening with age," said Gidjabolgo. "I could almost feel sorry for our Lord Forollkin. There is no sharper weapon than a woman's patience."

"And do I get a share of this new tenderness?"

"Tell me this before I answer," said Gidjabolgo. "Have you ever wanted to snap each bone in her slender body or tear out every silver hair? No? Then don't ask me for pity."

Kerish fumbled to detach a key and then tossed it to the Forgite.

"Lock the door behind you when you leave."

The Prince was still trembling when he reached the Galkian Room. He drew out and thumbed through volume after volume as he miserably debated with himself again over *The Book of Secrets*. Surely he shouldn't refuse any knowledge that might help their quest, but was that a good enough reason to break the Law of the Godborn? Pain stabbed through his crippled hand as if it still clasped the sharp-edged jewel; but the crystal cage was broken. Had the glory of Zeldin gone from him, or was it closer than ever now? Both thoughts frightened him. Kerish knelt by the window and tried to pray. How could he know what was right? Was it right to break the Law of the Godborn and read *The Book of Secrets*? Was it right to rob Vethnar of his key, his immortality? Was it right to search for the Promised Saviour at all?

A leaden calm engulfed him and the answers didn't seem to matter. Kerish stood up and looked across the crater. In the hazy distance the glorious creatures of the lake were transfixed by decay; but even that failed to move him. Suddenly he couldn't endure his own company any longer, but the thought of talking to Forollkin, Gwerath or Gidjabolgo was even more intolerable. Kerish-lo-Taan left *The Book of Secrets* where it lay and began to search for Llartian.

157

The Ellerinonn's rooms contained very little furniture but they were crowded with blocks of stone and half-finished sculptures. Llartian was working on one of these as he spoke to Rezag-Khal, who stood by a window that overlooked the sea. When Kerish entered, the Ellerinionn put down his chisel and shook the white stone-dust from his hands.

"Welcome, Prince."

"Oh, don't stop for me."

Kerish examined the half-carved head. The chin and the mouth were only just taking shape, but the thick brows, flaring nose and sharp cheekbones were already alive with Breldor's nervous intelligence.

"I have carved Vethnar and Dolodd already and as you see, Breldor is nearly finished. So, for purely selfish reasons, I was glad to hear that we had new guests. Would you let me try a likeness of you?"

Kerish didn't answer directly.

"Tell me, would you enjoy carving Gidjabolgo's portrait?"

"To be truthful – no. I fear my talents could not do justice to his . . . uniqueness. Will he be offended if I leave him out?"

Kerish's fingers traced the fall of Breldor's hair across the marble brow.

"I doubt it, though he will certainly pretend that he is. What about Rezag-Khal?"

"Ah, a fine strong face," said Llartian plaintively, "but he won't let me. He thinks I would trap his soul in the stone."

"Perhaps he's right."

Kerish crossed to the window.

"Rezag-Khal, how did the Khan's son die?"

"The Khan ordered me to teach the boy to ride. I chose the mare myself," answered Rezag-Khal. It was the one subject that he would always talk about. "The mare bolted and threw the Khan's son. He struck his head as he fell."

"I see, and what punishment do you deserve for this?"

"I deserve death."

"But you desire death, so how can it be a punishment? It seems to me that you take your crime too lightly."

In an instant the Chirazian's dagger was at his throat.

"Say so again and I will kill you, Galkian."

"So I am to be punished while you escape . . . Haven't you the courage to live and suffer to appease your Khan?"

"My blood is his appeasement."

Llartian stood poised to intervene, but Kerish said calmly, "Tell me, Rezag-Khal, what does your Khan hope for in death?"

"For the favour of Idaala and that his deeds should be remembered. His children's children will tell of them."

"But no-one beyond Chiraz will hear of these great deeds unless you speak of them," said Kerish. "If you told Vethnar, he would write them down, so that all over Zindar, century after century, men would read about your Khan. What better blood-gift could you offer your Lord?"

"What do you know of a warrior's deeds, crippled one?" demanded Rezag-Khal. "Have you ever split an enemy's skull with a broken shield or held back nine swordsmen in a narrow pass? *Men* would not read them." He rammed his dagger back in its sheath and marched out of the room.

Kerish smiled in self-mockery. He had set out from Galkis with such confidence, but in spite of the golden keys at his belt, he could not help one man to find a reason to live.

"He may think over what you've said," murmured Llartian. "It's always difficult to judge how he'll react. You never answered my question. I hope the answer is 'yes' because I don't often get a chance at bones like yours . . ."

"Oh, the portrait. No, I don't mind."

"Then let me sketch you first . . ." Llartian covered the half-finished head and searched for his reed brush and inks. "Sit there by the window, in the north light."

Kerish obeyed but just as Llartian had found a suitable scrap of vellum and had begun sketching the Prince's profile, Vethnar stalked in.

"Elmandis has tracked you down at last and now courteously asks for your return," announced the sorcerer. "So, Llartian, tomorrow you leave for home."

"Tomorrow! But I haven't . . ."

"The cage is open, no more bruising your wings against the bars; after all your complaints you might at least look pleased." He paced rapidly around the room and Llartian clutched at the carved head to protect it from the sorcerer's flying sleeves.

"If there's anything in your rooms that you like, take it away with you, though I'd be grateful if you'd leave that portrait of me behind. Tonight we shall hold a feast in your honour. Kerish, come with me."

Vethnar strode out of the room. Amused at Llartian's stunned expression, Kerish said gently, "Didn't you realize how much you liked him?" Without waiting for an answer he hurried after the sorcerer.

He had to take the stairs two at a time to catch up with Vethnar and he arrived beside him gasping for breath. A dark hand seized his good wrist and he couldn't help flinching as Vethnar thrust him towards a wall of rock. For a few seconds everything went black and he felt as if he were being turned inside out. Then he opened his eyes and said coldly, "I see. The keys you gave me open every door, but not every room has a door to open."

He found himself standing in a small, circular chamber. Its walls and ceiling were covered by a creeping plant whose variegated leaves shone with a dappled light. The plant was laden with flowers, but each one had a different colour, shape and scent, as if a whole garden was growing from one stem. Kerish hardly noticed it; his attention was fixed on a golden casket and the table on which it stood. From the rim of the table six hands seemed to grow. No, not six, five. One was no more than a tangle of charred bones, its ruined fingers still pointing upwards.

Chapter 9

The Book of the Emperors: *Chronicles*
*Then the Gentle God said to his son: "This is the last time
that I shall come to you in Galkis, for you no longer see me."
And Mikeld-lo-Taan cried out, "Father, I see you more clearly
than ever before. Your image is always before me!" "Beloved
child, it is that which hides me from you." Then Zeldin
departed from Zindar and was not seen again by men, walking
in the lands he loved.*

KERISH stared at the blackened hand, holding back
memories of Shubeyash but Vethnar leaned across the
table and touched a slender, copper-skinned hand. Its
fingers stirred into life and suddenly the copper hand was
gripping Vethnar's.

"Touch me!" commanded the sorcerer.

Kerish lightly clasped Vethnar's arm and the dappled
light faded into a cool shade. They seemed to be standing
between the pillars of a colonnade and somewhere close-by
a fountain was playing.

Damp with its spray, a man stepped from sunlight into
shadow. For a long moment Kerish stared into the
sea-green eyes of Elmandis. The once flaxen hair was now
bone white and the claws of Time had scarred the King of
Ellerinonn's face.

Then Vethnar tore his hand free and the vision faded.

"Do you understand now what your quest has done?"

"Thank you for showing me," said Kerish numbly. "I
knew that he would age, of course, once his key was gone,
but I never really imagined it happening."

"Elmandis is walking towards death again. What will
happen to fair Ellerinonn then?"

Kerish circled the table.

"By touching these hands, can you see any of the Seven
Sorcerers?"

161

"Yes, and talk with them too. Shubeyash and I devised the spell, many centuries ago. His dead fingers often summoned me, but I would not clasp them. Now it is too late." Vethnar gently stroked the blackened bones and Kerish looked away.

"Tell me, do you ever talk to Ellandellore?"

"That mischievous brat? Never. I do not care for children," said Vethnar, "and what should I have to say to him?"

"Let me see him now."

"Do you think this spell is a toy for your amusement . . ."

"No. Please raise Ellandellore. I promise that you won't find what you expect."

An appeal to the sorcerer's curiosity could not fail and Vethnar's long fingers closed around the smallest of the six hands. It was slow to respond but finally the copper flesh softened into life. Kerish touched Vethnar's arm and saw a boy, about twelve years old, seated on the grass beside a fountain. He was looking up at someone, listening intently, his heavy blond hair framing a face too solemn for his years. The man who was speaking laid a loving hand on the boy's shoulder and Ellandellore gazed trustingly at his brother. In the next second both of them became aware of the intrusion on their privacy. Elmandis's lips began to move but Vethnar snatched back his hand.

"The king of Ellerinonn has an heir," said Kerish. "Elmandis will die but Ellandellore will grow into wisdom. Ellerinonn may change but it won't be destroyed and it could be the same for you and for Tir-Melidon. Your pupils love you and I would never belittle the way you have chosen to use your power but why is your citadel so empty? If you let them, scholars would flock to Tir-Melidon from all over Zindar and death would not end your vision; they would be your heirs."

Vethnar backed away from him.

"Possibly, but is it likely that I will give up life while I enjoy every second of it?"

Kerish was still looking at the circle of hands.

"How long is it since you spoke to Saroc?"

162

"Not since you made him burn Tir-Tonar with all its wonders."

"And Sendaaka?"

"I never speak to her," said Vethnar harshly. "I shouldn't have brought you here, but I thought I could make you see . . ."

"Did you know that they're together now?" persisted Kerish. "He was your friend. Why not take his hand . . . or hers?"

"No."

"Can't you bear to see their happiness?" asked Kerish cruelly. "Or are you afraid to see what Time has done to her beauty?"

"Why should I care about either?" Vethnar paced towards the wall that had dissolved to let them enter.

"If you don't care," said Kerish, "why do you look at her portrait so often?"

For once the sorcerer stood quite still.

"The key was with the others but if you had entered the room I would have felt you lift the curtain."

"I didn't need to, Vethnar; you've seen Gwerath with my brother; you must know that I understand how you feel."

"I thought that I'd almost forgotten her," said Vethnar slowly, "but when I saw your Gwerath's silver hair . . . Sendaaka's mind was so like mine and we were searching for the same knowledge. One day on the cliffs of Gannoth we wove a spell together to transform ourselves into sea birds. I remember how it felt to swoop down and skim the waves and afterwards . . ."

"Vethnar, in this life she loves only Saroc but in Galkis the priests say that all desires are transmuted by the Gate of Death, that love can exist there without jealousy or . . ."

"And does that give you the slightest comfort now?" demanded Vethnar.

Kerish shook his head.

"No, and if I hadn't given my life to the search for the Saviour, I don't know how I could bear it. Vethnar, you must see that my quest is all I have; please help me!" The sorcerer sank down into a chair and sat with bowed head and Kerish knelt at his feet, waiting for an answer.

Gwerath and Forollkin were walking among the sombre trees that had reminded him of the woods above Galkis. Their feet made no sound on the drifts of needles as they followed the course of a shallow stream edged with pale, drooping ferns. Forollkin talked at unusual length about childhood in the Inner Palace and his training with the Imperial Guard. Finally, Gwerath broke through the barrier of words.

"And when you return to Galkis, when our quest is over, what will you do?"

"I suppose that depends on Kerish, what he chooses to . . ."

"Kerish, always Kerish! Why think of him?" demanded Gwerath. "You have your own life. What will you do with it?"

Forollkin stopped walking.

"I don't know. I've never had to think that far ahead."

"Well I do," said Gwerath. "I have lost my father, my tribe, my goddess; I have lost my past. I have to cling to the future. If we were still in Erandachu and I was still Torga of the Goddess, I would be the one to speak. I know that customs are different in Galkis but . . . Forollkin, surely you know why I left the Children of the Wind?"

Forollkin studied the ferns at his feet.

"I know that you wanted to be free of your circle, wanted to see Zindar . . ."

"Oh, sometimes I understand why Kerish stabbed you!" The anger in her voice finally made him look at her. "Go away," she said miserably, but it was she who ran, stumbling over the folds of her green dress.

"Zeldin brand me for a fool," muttered Forollkin. He strode after her, but not fast enough to catch her quickly.

Without noticing it, they had strayed close to the edge of the crater and suddenly a radiance moved through the woods. With a mighty rush of wings, one of the creatures of the lake ascended, its whole body singing. Golden fire burned in the veins beneath its pellucid skin and the glassy feathers struck against each other in a fierce complexity of sound. For a moment Gwerath stared at it and the harmonies blended into one clear, cold note like the cracking of ice.

"Gwerath, it's gone."

The Princess of the Sheyasa crouched in the shadow of a dead tree, her hands hiding her face.

"It's gone."

Forollkin knelt and put his arms around her.

"Gwerath, be angry, but please don't cry. At first I truly didn't realize why you'd come with us and later . . . Forgive me, I should have spoken before now." Through Gwerath's sobs he caught the one word "Pellameera". "It wasn't just her. I couldn't be sure of myself. I think I was afraid to be sure. Gwerath, I've always been shy of feelings I can't control, in myself or in anyone else and shy of making a future. Most of all I'm afraid of you and of what you might do to me, so I suppose I must love you."

Gwerath lifted her tear-blotched face from his shoulder.

"I loved you from the first moment I saw you at the Testing."

"Imarko alone knows why, and after the way I've treated you . . . Gwerath, I'm sorry I can't go as fast as you. Will you be patient with me for a little longer?" She nodded and Forollkin gently kissed her.

Kerish stood on the brow of a hill watching a day old kid trying out its spindly legs. Then he noticed Gidjabolgo crouching in a hollow, his knees thrust into his stomach and his shoulders heaving. Kerish ran towards him, the wind rippling his crimson robe and the black and silver of his hair.

"Gidjabolgo, are you ill?"

He knelt down anxiously but the Forgite straightened up and said in his usual manner, "No, my Master, I am merely suffering from a surfeit of surprises. First you and now the creatures of the lake. One of them flew above me. I'd looked at it before I could stop myself, but it didn't freeze." A reluctant wonder infused Gidjabolgo's voice. "I looked at the creature and it flew higher."

Kerish was beginning to understand how much that meant.

"Perhaps our journey has accomplished something then."

The bitter tone of his words made Gidjabolgo look at the Prince more closely.

"Is there nothing else to hope for from our journey? Have you grown tired of your grand quest?"

Kerish stared down at the clenched fingers of his useless hand.

"No, but my quest is impossible now. Vethnar will not give up his key. Gidjabolgo, I so nearly persuaded him. I used an unfair weapon against him and it almost worked. I thought I was going to win, but he still said no. I'd hurt him for nothing; everything I've done has been for nothing."

"And what will you do now?" asked the Forgite quietly. "Stay here and study, or slink back to Galkis?"

"I don't know, I haven't thought about it yet. I never really imagined that I could fail."

"Well there's a new task for you then; don't you remember Breldor's pretty speech on the inevitability of failure? Or doesn't it apply to the Godborn? Surely there's no need for you to take responsibility when you can claim that it's all the will of Zeldin?"

"It isn't like that . . ." began Kerish angrily.

"Then what is it like to be the child of a god? Tell me."

"It's no different from being you . . . Gidjabolgo, please help me!"

The Forgite looked into the eyes of the Godborn.

"Have you asked Vethnar why he won't look at the creatures of the lake?"

It was all he said and all Kerish needed him to say.

The travellers were summoned to Llartian's feast just before sunset. In honour of the Ellerinonn the table was spread with platters of colourful fruit and soft cheeses and bowls of cream and honey. Vethnar had changed into the least shabby of his brown robes and he had provided splendid new clothes for each of his guests. Kerish found the court dress of a Galkian prince spread out on his bed and wore it with his zeloka jewels. Only the suggestion that Gwerath might be pleased coaxed Forollkin into his new clothes but

Gidjabolgo cheerfully squeezed into his gaudy finery. For Gwerath herself the sorcerer had chosen a dress of black silk and strings of black pearls to wind in her silver hair.

Nine cups had been filled with wine and Vethnar raised his and said, "Let us drink to King Elmandis and to Llartian, whose departure we all regret, though it does give Dolodd an excuse to wear the curious finery of Dard."

Dolodd smiled, unperturbed. His grey hair was twisted into spiral curls trimmed with blue ribbons and jangling shells.

"I have never yet grown accustomed to it," continued Vethnar. "The origin of the shell decoration is rather interesting. The fifteenth Lord of Dard, Cevodd the Ill-tempered . . ."

"That's a long tale to listen to standing here with cups in our hands. Tell us to sit down."

"Ah, sensible Dolodd. Forgive me. To Elmandis and Llartian!"

The toast was drunk and they all sat down.

"You do want to go back?"

"Of course, Vethnar," said Llartian quickly.

"Good, good." The sorcerer offered him a bunch of glossy red fruit. "I should hate to make you act against your will. Forollkin, how magnificent you look; you should wear green more often. In Seld it's considered almost a crime for a man not to make himself as attractive as possible. A curious and most misguided race; but perhaps one of you would disagree? How disappointing."

Vethnar scooped the seeds from a plump fruit and sprinkled it with spice.

"When you return to Ellerinonn, what will you do first?"

"Pay my respects to the King," said Llartian. "Then I'll talk to my friends and find out what has been thought and written and sung and painted since I was away."

"And how long before you're sent into the world again?" asked Dolodd as he sliced up a cheese.

"We are usually given about three years between journeys," answered Llartian, "but it may be less if there is some special need for helpers in plague or famine or war."

"Then you may be banished from Ellerinonn again

sooner than you think," announced Vethnar. "This is a time of war." He turned to the Galkians. "I suppose I should have told you before, but it slipped my mind."

"The Five Kingdoms . . ."began Kerish."We knew that there was fighting in the territory beyond the Jenze . . ."

"The Khan of Orze has forced the Galkian army to retreat and all the land west of the river has fallen to him. Now he is mustering an even greater force and in spring they will cross the Jenze and attack Viroc. No, don't ask me for details, Forollkin, I know no more than that. Oh, except that the united fleets of Fangmere and Oraz are harrying the Galkian coast. Your journey home may be a dangerous one, Llartian, and I cannot protect you once you leave my territory."

"Once I reach the Sea of Az, I will trust in the protection of Elmandis."

Vethnar leaned back in his chair and studied the young Ellerionn.

"You think highly of Elmandis and his rule . . ."

"Yes, you won't find an Ellerinonn who doesn't."

"Breldor believes that failure is part of man's natural state." Gidjabolgo's chins scraped against his jewelled ruff as he spoke. "I claim that complaint is too. I am the greatest complainer of you all, so perhaps I am the most human. It seems to me that if none of Elmandis's subjects has any complaint, this king's power has deformed human nature itself and such a tyranny should be broken at any cost."

"You strike at what you cannot comprehend . . ." began Llartian, almost angrily, but Kerish intervened.

"I admire Elmandis but I suspect that Gidjabolgo may be right. The only way it can be tested is to see whether the people of Ellerinonn will continue to live in the same way when Elmandis is dead."

"Llartian, do you believe they would?"

For once, Vethnar sounded entirely serious. Llartian frowned and there was a long pause before he answered.

"If Elmandis were . . . no longer with us, I think my people would press for some changes. It would be good to be able to choose our own time for leaving Ellerinonn and at the moment we are forbidden to bring anyone from the

168

world beyond back with us, however much they might need our care . . ."

"Elmandis is a jealous lover of his Kingdom," said Vethnar quietly, "and of his people."

"No one blames him but . . ."

"But, you are going to claim that, given freedom, you would serve King and Kingdom more ardently than ever. I have lived long enough to doubt that kind of reasoning. However," Vethnar deftly skinned a crimson fruit, "I comfort myself with the thought that people are always complaining about me, so I should escape Gidjabolgo's disapproval."

"You could do something rarer and earn his praise," suggested Kerish, "if you will grant Gidjabolgo one wish. I promise you that he has earned his desire."

"Nevertheless, there must still be a price; that is one rule that even I recognize. Name your wish," ordered Vethnar, "and we will debate it. If everyone here agrees that it should be granted, then it will be."

"No," exclaimed Kerish. "Name another condition!"

"The Prince has tried for so long to bridle my tongue that he has forgotten that I have one," said Gidjabolgo sharply. "On such terms I want nothing from you or from anyone."

"Your desire cannot be very strong," murmured Vethnar.

"I am practising to become a model of graceful resignation with my lot," answered the Forgite.

Vethnar looked unconvinced.

"Can resignation ever be a virtue?"

"Many people have thought so." Dolodd ladled cream over his plate of fruit. "Perhaps the test lies in how hard it is to practise."

"I think resignation is a vice," interrupted Breldor. "To strive, even when there is no hope . . . that is true virtue!"

"It seems to me," responded Llartian, "to be the height of foolishness."

He began to elaborate on this opinion, but not everyone was listening.

Forollkin was staring at Gwerath, perturbed by her dark

splendour and wishing her back in her usual boy's clothes. Gwerath herself was troubled by the Chirazian, who sat in silence, eating nothing. Almost as if she was afraid of her own happiness, she felt compelled to try and give some of it away.

"Do your people worship a goddess?" she asked.

Rezag-Khal touched his brow in a gesture of reverence. "We worship Idaala, the Lady of Blood."

"Then in her name, I command you to eat."

She picked up a crimson-skinned fruit and offered it to him. Rezag-Khal stared at her for a moment and then took the fruit and bit into the sweet flesh beneath the tart crimson skin.

Meanwhile the discussion had taken several twists and turns and Breldor was declaring, "Surely, it is better to simply refuse to recognize an obstacle than to deceive yourself by belittling it."

"You can refuse to recognize a pile of dung," put in Gidjabolgo "but you'll still smell foul when you've stepped in it."

"Breldor," began Dolodd more gently. "This hardly seems consistent with your insistence that we should all strive without hope."

"Oh, but it is!" Absurdly excited, Breldor banged down his cup for emphasis and red drops beaded the cloth. "Failure is inescapable but what could be grander than to refuse to recognize it, to persist in trying to impose our own order on the world."

"Men certainly do that," agreed Vethnar. "It is their gravest fault, but it makes them more interesting than any of their virtues."

Kerish had been silent for a long time, but now he leaned forward and said, "Vethnar, you were born human. Amongst your great store of knowledge is there no room to remember what it felt like?"

The sorcerer was absently squeezing the spines from a bulbous yellow fruit, squirting his neighbours with juice. He did not look up.

"I am gifted with an excellent memory."

"In our travels," continued Kerish, "we have heard a

great deal about 'Forbidden Knowledge'. None of the sorcerers whom we've met has been eager to disclose the nature of his power or the effect that it has had on him."

Vethnar snorted.

"I can imagine, but *I* have never cloaked myself in mysteries. It is true that some of our knowledge is dangerous to humans, as dangerous as handing a torch to a savage who knew nothing of fire. He would soon learn its nature but only through the pain of burning. As long as you understand the risk ask anything you like."

Kerish pushed back his chair and got up from the table. Gold and silver embroidery glittered in the stiff folds of his cloak of Imperial purple and the starflowers of his coronet seemed as dark and lustrous as the ones that grew in the Valley of Silence. Watching him, Forollkin suddenly felt that his brother was more dangerous than Vethnar would ever be. In the same moment Llartian decided that he could never have captured the Prince's likeness in stone and Dolodd turned an oddly tender look on the sorcerer.

"When you were granted your key," began Kerish, "how did it change your nature?"

"It made me immortal," answered Vethnar, "and because of that I see everything in a different way. You must look at the world from the one place where you stand, but I see it as if through the windows of a great tower. Every few steps there is a new window and a new view of Zindar and I can go on climbing for ever."

Kerish nodded.

"I agree that you see things differently because of your immortality but, as far as I can judge, it is a kind of sight that does nothing but hinder your great task of gathering knowledge about Zindar . . ."

"Hinder! How can you . . ."

"Please let me finish, Vethnar. Firstly, your very confidence in yourself has stopped you seeking the help you need; stopped you filling Tir-Melidon with people who could add to your knowledge and profit from it."

"No sense of urgency," muttered Dolodd. "If I've said it once, I've said it a thousand times."

"Secondly," said Kerish, "you are fascinated by people

because you find it so difficult to understand them. However many conversations you record, however many captives you interrogate, however many books you read – you will not be an inch near understanding men as long as you keep your immortality. The knowledge of death shapes our humanity and until you share that knowledge from the inside, people will remain a puzzle to you, however hard you study us."

Kerish moved away from the table, his crippled hand held high against his heart.

"Thirdly, however high your tower, your view is not really so different from that of the man on the ground. It is only a matter of degree; you still have only one man's vision."

"No, indeed," protested Vethnar, "within my territory I can see and hear whatever I choose. I am not restricted by my body."

"No, but you are by your mind. You are not limited by what you see, but by the means you have to interpret it."

The Prince brushed strands of damp hair from his forehead.

"The evening is rather warm; do you mind if I open a window?"

There was a sudden and complete silence. Breldor looked down at his hands but Rezag-Khan stopped chewing and stared curiously at the sorcerer. Golden grains drifted across the table as Vethnar shook out some spice.

"Why not? You must forgive me. Though I detest Kolgor, I must admit that I was born a southerner and I'm used to the desert heat. Gwerath, as a child of the cold north, I hope you haven't been too uncomfortable. You should have spoken up."

Gwerath merely smiled at him, so the sound of the Prince fumbling with the window catch was clearly audible.

"Your questions are very modest, Kerish," continued Vethnar, "and what you say is really most interesting."

The Prince stood with his back to the table, looking out across the crater.

"You said a little while ago that trying to impose our own order on the world was mankind's greatest fault. I take it," said Kerish, "that your aim is to study the true order."

"Of course."

"Given eternity, I can see that you might be able to gather all the pieces of the puzzle, but are you sure that you can fit them together?"

"You said yourself that I have passed beyond the reason that makes men try to force the pieces into false patterns."

"Passed beyond or retreated from?" Kerish turned, smiling apologetically. "I'm afraid I can't open this one-handed. Will you help me?"

"Breldor, help the Prince to . . ."

"No," said Kerish. "I was always taught that a good commander never gave an order which he would be reluctant to carry out himself."

"No doubt. So?"

"So, can the Sorcerer of Tir-Melidon not open a window?"

"I could. I could also sweep the floor and wash the dishes, but I'd be of little use to Zindar if I wasted my time on such things."

"You refuse then?"

"No!"

Vethnar angrily slammed back his chair, strode across the room and pulled down the catch. He pushed the window open without glancing through its panes but Kerish gripped his shoulder.

"Vethnar, look out of the window you have opened."

An irridescent turquoise light, veined with gold, shimmered through the glass as one of the creatures of the crater flew close to the window.

"What is the use of your lofty tower if you can't outclimb fear?" asked Kerish. "I stand on the ground. I know that I can't see clearly enough and I weep for it, but I am not afraid."

Vethnar had moved away but the light streaked across his face and the room vibrated with a sound like the roar of a waterfall.

"Please," said Kerish, "please look."

Very slowly, Vethnar turned towards the splendour. Twelve fiery turquoise wings beat out an intricate rhythm

173

and at their centre was an eyeless face full of mouths opened in song. Kerish knew as he looked at it that all his life he had misinterpreted beauty; this was far more lovely than any human face.

For a long moment Vethnar trembled with joy but the harmonies that were the creature's voice were too complex to be endured; already his mind was breaking them up into parts small enough for him to grasp. Abruptly the great wings were stilled, the crystalline lips whitened and the music dissolved into discord and died away.

The creature hung motionless before him, not beautiful, but grotesque and Vethnar covered his face and wept.

Kerish gently led the sorcerer back to the table and knelt beside his chair.

"Vethnar. I am certain that neither of us will ever understand the pattern while we are still part of it. By taking immortality you have lost more than you gained."

"When I left Kolgor," the sorcerer's muffled voice was still thick with tears, "the Chief of the Elders said to me, 'Vethnar, however much you take from the world, you will never achieve your desire because you are incapable of receiving.' All my long life I have tried to prove him wrong, but it seems that I can't."

"It is only the fierceness of your desire for truth that makes it impossible for you to accept something that your mind cannot classify. You destroy such visions as you study them and because you are wise and good, Vethnar, you know how much you are losing."

"It is a wound that cannot be staunched," said Dolodd quietly, "but it makes leaving this world a little less painful. You know that I've made my decision; why don't you give the Prince what he wants and then perhaps we can get down to some real work."

"But for how long?" asked Vethnar.

"For ever," answered Dolodd. "When we're gone, Breldor will go on gathering the pieces. Knowledge always has an heir."

"Breldor, come here." The sorcerer uncovered his face and Breldor hurried to his side, frowning with anxiety. "Could you rule my citadel?"

"Not as you do, Vethnar, but I love Tir-Melidon and I want to spend my life here."

"And if I summoned scholars from all over Zindar to work in Tir-Melidon, could you rule them?"

"I hope, on important matters, that I could persuade them to agree with me."

"And to disagree, always remember that. It may be just as vital . . . Oh, I'm sorry, Kerish." The sorcerer's sweeping gesture had almost knocked the Prince over. He smiled as he regained his balance.

"You really mean that and I suppose that's why you escaped the fate of Shubeyash."

"The wound you spoke of hurt him more than any of us," answered Vethnar. "His solution was to try and split apart his mind and his body. His freedom trapped him in a worse prison and what he saw through his new eyes de—stroyed him. Llartian, you look as though you haven't understood a single word we've said."

"I haven't," admitted Llartian, "but I feel that I've learnt from it all the same."

"And, Forollkin," continued the sorcerer, in almost his normal voice, "you are sitting there very quietly beside Gwerath but, as I recall, you are the one for blunt speeches and direct questions. Your brother is too courteous to rush me, so you will have to do the asking."

"For your key? Vethnar, will you give us your key?"

"There is now a possibility that I might." Vethnar picked the last fruit from the bowl and polished it on his sleeve. "Perhaps I would become more amenable if you favoured us with that speech on the nature of heroism . . . ah don't look so agonized, Forollkin. Yes, I will give you my key."

A dawn mist hung over the lake as the travellers left Tir-Melidon. The walk down the slope was like descending into a vast temple, filled with half-hidden spendours and echoing with sacred music. They glimpsed occasional flashes of gold or azure and knew that all around them the great dance was continuing.

As they reached the shore, Vethnar began to upbraid

175

Dolodd for failing to look sad.

"Partings deserve tears. In Kolgor they tried to make me keep the same bland expression whether I was burying my best friend or discovering the secrets of Zindar. I would have none of it. Now Breldor here looks properly gloomy, but you men of Dard have no feelings. I suppose it comes from earning a fat living from strangling chicks and selling their feathers. You can't expect sensitivity from a race who . . ."

"Perhaps you could itemize our national failings another morning," said Dolodd patiently. "Your guests are anxious to be off."

Vethnar apologized, bowing so low that his heavy sleeves brushed the wet sand.

"Board your boat then. I have re-provisioned her and woven a few spells around her. When you're satisfied that I haven't forgotten anything vital, you might care to invite us aboard to drink to a safe journey."

All the storm damage had been set to rights and the cabin of the *Starflower* was crammed with chests of provisions. A new hammock had been slung for Llartian who was to travel with them part of the way to Ellerinonn. When his meagre luggage had been loaded, everyone sat down on the rugs spread across the *Starflower*'s deck. Vethnar shifted uncomfortably, trying to keep his long legs out of everyone's way as Gwerath handed round a platter of flower-shaped spice biscuits and Forollkin poured out eight goblets of wine.

"Well, Llartian, I hope you've got the letter for Elmandis."

Llartian patted the pouch at his waist.

"It's here, Vethnar, and I think I can remember all your last minute additions and changes."

"Good, good. Tell your countrymen about Tir-Melidon, without Elmandis finding out, if you can, and assure them that they would be welcome to study here."

"And my countrywomen?" asked the Ellerinionn "Would they be welcome too?"

The sorcerer looked alarmed and turned to Breldor.

"What do you say to that?"

176

"Anyone who loves learning must be welcome," said Breldor loftily. "I shall not notice if they are young or old, men or women."

"Most commendable," murmured Dolodd, "and quite impossible."

Kerish noticed that his name was written on the petals of a cake shaped like a starflower. Forollkin had eaten three before Kerish could bring himself to bite into his.

"I think it would be best," Vethnar was saying, "if you landed Llartian on Cheransee. Then the black boat of Ellandellore will ferry him safely across the Straits of Rac and you will have lost no time on your journey."

"Our journey to where?" asked Forollkin.

"Perhaps I had better answer that question when you have my key. Dolodd, where did I put it?"

"In your sleeve; no, the left one."

Vethnar rummaged through his sleeve, expressions of surprise and distaste flitting across his face until finally he produced a golden casket. Kerish tugged out the chain from about his waist and Gidjabolgo helped him detach the dark-gemmed key of Tir-Roac.

"Hurry," snapped the sorcerer. "Oh, let me do it!"

Impatiently, Vethnar unlocked the casket and placed the sixth key, set with a rich brown gem, on Kerish's palm. Inarticulate for once, the Prince tried to thank the sorcerer, but Vethnar cut him short.

"Now, for the seventh citadel you must go back to Galkis."

"Galkis! But there are no sorcerers there!"

"If you *had* chosen to read *The Book of Secrets*, Prince, no doubt you would have found the truth there. A few of your legends echo it. In the Jungle of Jenze you will find Tir-Jenac, the citadel of the sorceress Tebreega."

"There is the legend of Prince Il-Keno and the evil enchantress of Jenze but . . . ."

"A pretty story," said Vethnar, "and you need not think Il-Keno a liar. He was sworn to silence by Tebreega and he had no power over the imaginations of the legend-weavers of Joze. Forget their version if you can."

Kerish was glad to try, for it carried with it memories of

177

Gankali's murder.

"To my knowledge, no other Galkian has entered the Forbidden Jungle of Jenze. How shall we find Tir-Jenac?"

Vethnar asked for another cup of wine and leaned back against a coil of rope.

"When you reach the edge of the jungle, no matter where, follow the first path you meet and never stray from it. Then you will be bound to find Tir-Jenac. Tebreega did not choose to live in the jungle because she wished for solitude; far from it, as you will see. Now listen carefully, don't linger in large open spaces, though the pools are safe enough. If you lose your way, hang a gift on a tree and the chattering birds that sit on every bough will be your guides. Yellow and scarlet fruits are the ones to eat, leave the green alone and never touch discarded feathers. It might be best to laugh aloud and if you make music — well, I don't say that it's dangerous but your journey won't be as peaceful as it might be." Vethnar took a gulp of wine.

"I think that's all I have to warn you about. I've written it down on a scroll tied with a red ribbon. It might be by the spice chest or under Forollkin's pillow or in the . . . but, no, that's not visible yet. Llartian, thank you for leaving my portrait. I can't think that my nose really looks like that but it will do to overawe feasts in the Debating Chamber when I am gone. Amongst your luggage you will find a chisel that will cut the hardest stone as if it were cheese. I wanted to add a block of Kolgorn marble, the veining is exquisite . . ."

"But I wouldn't let him," put in Dolodd. "The boat is overloaded as it is."

"What will you do with Rezag-Khal?" asked Llartian.

"I shall keep him here for three months longer," answered the sorcerer, "and then release him, to his death if he chooses, but Gwerath has given me some new ideas about how to tempt him to live. That kid was female by the way, did you notice? I shall call it after you, Princess. Now you will find sundry small gifts in your cabin and to you, Gidjabolgo, my present is an untroubled voyage. As long as your boat is in the Dirian Sea just lash the helm and let her take her own course."

"And if the course she chooses takes us into a storm?"

"Ah, well as to that . . ." A curious expression half-way between shame and pride crossed Vethnar's face. "I needed a little time to think before I finally gave up my key, so last night you all slept for rather longer than you realized. Beyond Silnarnin it is early spring and you will meet nothing but fair winds and gentle seas. Dolodd, Breldor . . . we must get back to work."

The sorcerer stood up and pointed.

"Do you see that tunnel in the rock face, to the left of the one you entered from? Let the *Starflower* take you through it. To the east of Silnarnin lie their gardens and quiet places, so it's not a maze of rock like the central city."

"How long has the city been under the sea?" asked Gwerath.

"Since before men came into Zindar," answered Vethnar. "This island was forbidden ground to them, except that once in their lives each citizen had to enter the crater. I doubt if they ever talked about what they saw there."

"And were the people all drowned with their city?" asked Forollkin.

"No, they moved eastwards and the city was deserted long before the sea covered it. I have my own ideas about why they left, but your guesses are as good as mine. Goodbye, Kerish."

The Prince's right hand clasped the sorcerer's.

"I haven't really thanked you for your kindness . . ."

"It wasn't kindness. As you said, people fascinate me and the key . . ." Vethnar paused. "Your arguments compelled me to give it to you and there's no virtue in acting under compulsion."

Breldor opened his mouth to disagree and Kerish said quickly, "No. Your choice was made freely and we honour you for it."

The rest of their farewells were soon over and Vethnar and his companions jumped ashore. As they began the steep climb back to Tir-Melidon Vethnar leaned on Breldor's shoulder and was heard to complain that the cold was seeping into his aging bones. Dolodd retorted that by human reckoning Vethnar was barely thirty and could expect no sympathy yet.

179

The *Starflower* slid away from the shore as one of the creatures of the lake swept overhead with a noise like a forest of bronze shaken by storms. The mist was thinning now and they passed under the body of a second creature whose frozen coils glittered like a torrent of green ice in the morning sunlight. Glancing back, Kerish saw that Vethnar had paused beside the great creature whose final agony spread across the slope. He was staring somberly at it, as if he could see the ruined face beneath the flood of golden hair. Then Vethnar turned again towards the crater and waved at the *Starflower* as cheerfully as a child, his sleeves slapping the wind.

The voyage from Silnarnin to Cheransee was as calm and uneventful as the sorcerer had promised. With little sailing to do and no excuse to shout at Forollkin, Gidjabolgo spent many hours playing the Prince's zildar and often accompanied Kerish as he sang for the others, when the cool evenings drove them below long before they were ready to sleep. He refused to teach Gwerath and since Kerish could no longer demonstrate the correct fingerings, her music made little progress. In reading and writing however her skill increased rapidly and Forollkin helped Kerish to teach her High Galkian, the ancient language of the Emperor's Court. Vethnar's gifts had included some Galkian books which Kerish was pleased to use for the reading lessons.

Not all of the sorcerer's presents were so practical. He had forgotten some essentials and filled the water barrels with wine. An inordinate amount of space was taken up by a chest of Kolgorn spices, but nobody complained when a fruit tree suddenly sprouted from the deck. Gwerath was delighted to discover a flask of steaming peshlinn that was always full, no matter how much you drank, and every morning they were woken by the song of a golden bird. It would perch on each of the travellers' pillows until someone touched it with a sleepy hand and then it would vanish until the next day. At night they needed no lanterns. A sweet-scented plant had twined itself about the rigging and its creamy flowers gave out a gentle light. Its leaves rustled through the hours of darkness and only Kerish could

180

distinguish in that sound the voice of Vethnar whispering protective spells.

Llartian proved a congenial travelling companion. He joined in the High Galkian lessons and in return offered stories about Elmandis and about famous journeys by generations of his subjects into the dark places of Zindar. He and Kerish had long debates on the merits of the art and literature of Galkis and Ellerinonn and sometimes combined to defend them both against attacks by Gidjabolgo. Forollkin and Gwerath were never actually alone together but, when watching them talking, sometimes Kerish felt that they had forgotten his existence.

All too soon the tranquil voyage was over and Cheransee was in sight. Forollkin plied his brother with questions about the Isle of Illusions, but Kerish's memories were of the screaming Rocks and the blue tower of Tir-Racneth and he could only shake his head.

"I hardly saw the island as it really is, so I can't describe it."

While Gidjabolgo guided the *Starflower* through dangerous shallows to the southern shore of Cheransee, Kerish stood beside him remembering the one illusion that still haunted him; his own image.

They landed in a quiet cove and Llartian splashed ashore, eager to cross the narrow island, to find Tir-Racneth and the black boat that would take him home. Kerish imagined the blue tower standing open, its treasures scattered to wind and rain. Tir-Racneth desolate, Tir-Tonar burned . . . what else would he have to destroy before his quest was over and the Saviour was freed?

When they were all standing on the white beach, Llartian embraced Kerish.

"Goodbye and good fortune in your quest, whatever it may be. Have you any message for Elmandis?"

"Tell him he was right to hate me."

"No." Llartian's hands tightened on Kerish's shoulders and he shook his flaxen head.

"No, I won't tell him that because it can't be true."

"Then simply say that I will try not to betray his trust."

Forollkin and Gwerath went part of the way with

Llartian and raced back across the moorland together, arriving laughing and breathless. They spent a peaceful night in the cove and sailed just before dawn. By the next day they were through the Straits of Rac and into the Sea of Az. The flowers on the rigging faded, the fruit tree withered and they were no longer woken by birdsong. Vethnar's protection went no further and Gidjabolgo complained bitterly at having to sail the *Starflower* again. Forollkin and Gwerath worked hard to help him and got no thanks for it. In their different ways all three of them tried not to make Kerish feel useless, but there was little for him to do but lie in his hammock thinking back over their journey.

One afternoon he came on deck to hear Forollkin telling Gwerath about the islands known as the Footsteps of Zeldin.

"He was a giant then?" asked Gwerath teasingly. "I thought you said that he was a young man with purple and black and golden eyes, just like Kerish."

"He is in most statues and paintings," admitted Forollkin, "but I suppose he can change his size at will."

Gwerath relented.

"It was the same with the Hunter of Souls. Sometimes he was only the size of a man but when he hunted the West Wind he was the tallest thing in Erandachu. As he ran after his quarry he kept hitting his head against stars and knocking them out of the sky and where they fell mountains sprang up. I remember my father telling me the story when I was little and pretending to be the Hunter getting excited and bumping into the stars."

"A pious education no doubt," muttered Gidjabolgo. "Do these Footsteps of yours have any fresh water, my Masters?"

Kerish nodded.

"Each of the islands has a spring; Zeldin's gift to travellers."

Gidjabolgo steered the *Starflower* into the nearest cove. They took on water and anchored there for the night and in the morning the ships of Fangmere caught them.